# THE ROGUE REFRAIN
## ELORA TUNE: BARD AT LARGE TWO

# PATTI LARSEN
## USA TODAY BESTSELLING AUTHOR

Thanks, Kirstin!

ISBN-13: 978-1-998948-59-8

# CHAPTER ONE

Pennywhistle huffed a soft nicker as he shifted his weight from one back foot to the other, nudging Twinkletoes gently with his soft muzzle. I offered the big chestnut gelding a soft pat to his neck in comfort, though he was content enough to wait.

I was the impatient one, doing my best to hide it, slouching comfortably in my saddle and running the lyrics of a new song in my head to keep from sighing deeply at the stagnant linc of folk waiting to pass through the tall wooden gates of Vorentine.

"Seriously," Fig muttered, my best friend's pointed lack of outward poise and calm not helping matters. Fig Marigold might have been new to the trail, her first full adventure with a real company just behind her, but she'd taken on a rather amusing swagger I wasn't sure she'd earned. That had her a bit grumpier than I was used to from the former housegnome and widow, long gone the days of her tending the garden and her beloved husband, Fennel. Now a blooded warrior (snort) she'd adopted the kind of self-assured confidence I usually attributed to those with years in the field.

While there was reason for that attitude to make me anxious, I chose to see it otherwise. Not that I'd openly tease her about it. Fig had waited her whole life to join me on the road and only did so after her sweet partner passed away just a short time ago. Still, I worried she might have already lost her kind nature, her wide-eyed enthusiasm and innocence and the ability to see things with a sense of wonder that made Fig so irresistibly adorable to everyone she knew.

Not that naivete would serve her out here, mind you, but who said that was a good thing?

She looked up at me, flicking her long, blonde bangs out of her pale green eyes, the thick braids she'd chosen to wear over both shoulders wound tight with leather cords. Whoever taught her that trick hadn't talked her into cutting her hair off just yet, though I knew that was coming. Even if my oldest friend wasn't utterly attached to her impressive golden locks, there would come a time that some ambitious goblin would wield a cunning dagger too close, or a reaching ogre catch one of those heavy plaits in a fist to force her to decide between her vanity and her life.

As it was, she had the tip of one braid in her gloved hands, toying with the curve of it, her anxious fiddling only making her small dapple pony squeal and snap at her trail partner. My poor horse flinched back, shaking his head, though I knew her effort had only been halfhearted.

Fig grunted at her pony before eye rolling with her tenth giant inhale and exhale of the last quarter-hour. "How much longer? We have things to *do*."

Her eager annoyance made me smile, if only a little, as I reached for my waterskin and took a sip, fortunate that my elf heritage allowed me to use a bit of magic to lower my body temperature. Otherwise, the blazing heat of the midday sun would have made this wait even more miserable. And yes, I extended that power out to my horse, my best friend and her pony as well, so no judging. Yes, that meant the rest of the sullen and unhappy line had to suffer, but I didn't have to spend any amount of time with them past this point and listening to Fig snark about being hot just wasn't something I wanted to add to her repertoire.

I wasn't above using my power for my own advantage, even if doing so might draw the wrong kind of attention. I was far too careful to allow that, thank you.

"I'm sure it won't be much longer," I said, just as the wagon ahead of us suddenly lurched forward, the driver calling out to the pair of mules pulling its creaking, complaining bulk past the tall guards inspecting everyone who passed them. I didn't have to guide Pennywhistle to avoid the small cascade of what looked like turnips that bounced free of the back of the man's wagon, though Fig was vocal enough when

Twinkletoes danced sideways to do the same.

"Litterbug," she muttered.

"You know," I said, "you could have stayed with your company and gone back into the Everwilding." I didn't mean it the way it sounded, so don't take that tone with me. If anything, I was happy for her that she'd connected with a group that she seemed comfortable enough with to not only depart from me past the border (I didn't worry much) and then return to me (all right, fine, I worried a lot) with bright eyes and a big smile and a small pouch of gold to pad her purse in payment for fetching some relic or another (bad friend, no interest in details). Not everyone who chose the adventuring life in the monster-infested reaches of the Everwilding just beyond the safety of our home kingdom of Valoria returned. In fact, the statistics were dismal. Thus my concerns and pride in her for her success.

So, my reason for commenting wasn't to get rid of her. I was happy to have her back. She'd already indicated that she'd consider adventuring with them again if she seemed hesitant to commit. But if she was anxious and trying to hide it behind this façade she'd adopted, maybe another jaunt—tossed back into the fire, as it were—might be just the thing she needed.

Which presented its own set of concerns, but I was trying not to think about that.

Fig wrinkled her nose at me, shoulders back and face settling as we came even with the two guards. "Afternoon," she said, taking over the conversation before I could speak, surprising me with her aggressive tone. "Fig Marigold and Elora Tune, at your service."

"Papers." The guard on the right, the one next to me, sounded bored and looked hot under his heavy helmet. Whoever dressed these poor sods in chainmail and plate embellishments with full dark velvet surcoats and leather breaches either had a sick and cruel sense of humor or had never stood in the hot sun in full regalia before. Mind you, these two weren't official Guards, not of royal make, anyway. Their badges were minted from some merchant guild, again not the Guild of which I was most accustomed, tied to the Royal Family and all the rules and regulations that went with it. I hadn't been to Vorentine in almost a decade, choosing to avoid small cities this size, but I was low on some things that I really needed and couldn't get in the smaller centers I preferred. Which meant this was our only option.

An option that Fig seemed determined to cross off the very short (city of one, excuse me) list at our disposal.

"Do you know who this is?" She jerked her thumb in my direction and now I really wished she had gone with the group and not for the right reasons.

"El something, something," he said. "Papers."

Fig inhaled to humiliate me further only to jerk to a stop when I kicked her firmly, grateful Twinkletoes chose to stay close to Pennywhistle so I didn't have to make a fool of myself to do so.

"Good sir," I said, reaching into my saddlebag for my credentials, Fig rummaging with a grumble for hers, "as requested." I handed the stamped parchment inside its leather folder over, my sullen friend doing the same. "With thanks for your service."

He shot my friend a frown but seemed to soften when I stroked his ego. "Business in Vorentine?"

"She's a bard," Fig snapped. "What do you think she's doing here?"

By the Blessed Light of Theridion Himself, if she didn't stop, I was going to strangle her. "I am, indeed," I said, "as you can see by the stamp on my paperwork. Elora Tune, Bard at Large."

He squinted at the page and I instantly leaped to the understanding that the man couldn't decipher the writing there since he'd never learned to do so. Which only made things worse when he looked up at me, dark eyes meeting mine. "Out of?"

That information was also on the paperwork. Something Fig knew. A question I should have anticipated and yet, one that took me by surprise only because I made the mental leap to his lack of education in the same instant that I should have been prepared for my diminutive fighter friend's attack of attitude.

"Yinderfell, duh," she said as I choked. "Can't you read?"

We were never getting through those gates now, were we?

## CHAPTER TWO

My normally quick wit and ability to reshape unfortunate situations felt like a losing battle in this instance as I watched the man's face flush even darker behind the grooved mask of his helmet. What little was visible of his cheeks under the metal and heavy beard beneath was so purple suddenly that I feared he might actually keel over.

Instead, he slapped the paperwork into my outstretched hand and snarled at me.

"Denied," he growled.

Just great. "Good sir," I said.

"You did not just—" Fig huffed.

"Enough!" The guard's anger wasn't backing down and my gnome friend was a big (small but mighty) part of that troublesome rage. "This isn't some royal squat," he said with deep condescension that had her spluttering, "in some pampered part of the kingdom." It sounded like he thought less of anyone who lived further from the border than he did, a typical attitude, truth be told, for those who chose to exist this close to the Everwilding and its continual risks. "This is a *merchant* city," he said, chest out, shoulders back, as his fellow on the Fig's side did the same. "A freehold, by law and the word of those who live here. You could be the queen herself," he told me, "and you'd be turning your fancy rear end around and leaving my sight because neither of you is fit to pass through our gates."

That, as they say, was that then. I knew better than to argue. If anything, I usually did my very best to butter up and joke with the gate guards when necessary, to ensure I was on their good side. After this long wait in the heat, however, a wasted almost full turn of the hourglass, I'd come to realize that my little gnome friend wasn't playing by the same rules as I was.

Or the same humility by necessity.

Something she proved by standing up in her stirrups and half-turning toward the waiting line while I cringed and was again far too late to stop her before she raised her voice and fist in the air.

"Is this the kind of greeting you give to visitors in Vorentine?"

Oh, Fig. Figgle Figgy Figusta. That *tone*. A perfect match to his, but loud enough for it to carry all the way to the back of the line. Not to mention forward, to the six other guards screening various categories of traveler—those on foot, on wheels and carrying goods—all of whom turned toward us and stared while she spoke even louder (I kid you *not*, dear friend, because clearly, they hadn't heard her through the city walls yet). "Shame on you," she said in a droning thunder of a judgment fit for a paladin of the Light. "*Shame*, I say."

Now, had that come from my giant and gregarious brother, Thune Yestervere, as the head of the paladin Order of Light and Liberty, perhaps it would have gained us access. The trouble was, despite her best effort, Fig's delivery lacked a certain oomph that an Oath to a God like the ever-watching Theridion commanded. Instead, as a heavy and increasingly awkward pause ensued, I wished the ground would open up and swallow me whole.

Would have paid a lot of money for a portal just then.

The guard's pike twitched in his hand and now things were getting out of control. But as I inhaled to intervene and keep my gnome friend from ushering in her doom at the pointed end of a sharp and long-reaching blade, we were interrupted.

Thank the gods and stars for small mercies.

A young man in the same dark velvet as the guards staggered his way through the gate and made his way toward us, drawing focus with his weaving walk and inability to stay upright without various armored folk to prop him up as he went. His arrival at Pennywhistle's nose ended in a squinted frown up at me, then at Fig and finally at the furious guard who'd turned us away.

A guard who now stared at the ground with a frown barely visible but now bowing under the interest of this rather drunken young man. In bad need of a haircut, a change of doublet—even if it looked expensive—and a long sleep to knock the edge off his inebriation.

And yet, he seemed capable of thought, it seemed, because he addressed the guard with most of his words coherent and in an order that made enough sense that I understood him.

"Trouble, dear boy? Trouble indeed. Why are they stopped? They need to move again, you see."

"Master Vorentine," the guard began, but the young man—a Vorentine himself, as luck would have it, related, I could only assume, to the city's namesake—looked up at me, waving at the open gate.

"Why aren't you?" He floundered and I rescued him in a careful and kindly tone.

"Moving, sir?" I glanced down at the guard who inhaled to speak only to talk over him. With a very fast grab for Fig this time, not giving her a moment to interfere thanks to a hard pinch that had her rubbing her skin and frowning at me. "We were just about to, thank you, Master Vorentine. Your kind guards were giving us that instruction." I focused on the guard who glared back at me. "So we don't hold up the line."

"Very good, very good, yes, perfect, move along." The young man's gestures disturbed even my trail-steady horse to the point that Pennywhistle snorted and sidestepped, Twinkletoes just fast enough to prevent him walking into her. That meant the guard beside Fig had to dodge and we were suddenly in motion, the young man speaking to the two soldiers while I ground my teeth together and didn't yell at my friend.

Yet. Yell at my friend, *yet*. That would be happening the second we were safely away from the gate and in private. Except she started up again, didn't she? This time chattering on and on about how that showed them and wasn't he just a fool and other things my brain couldn't process because I was so.

Freaking.

Angry.

I made it three streets into the city before I spun on her, Fig's smug expression and steady stream of words dying in the same instant, her pale green eyes huge in her round face as I hissed at her.

"I have no idea what *that* was," I snapped, jabbing a finger back in the direction we'd come, "but if you *ever*," I had to breathe before I could speak again, "put me in that position," another breath was necessary, "*ever* again, Fig," I had to fist my hand against my thigh while my gelding bounced under me in anxiety over my upset, "I will personally strangle you and toss your body in the Everwilding." I let out a short, furious exhale. "Are we clear?"

She blinked. Nodded. Sagged in her saddle. "Sorry," she whispered. "I don't know what got into me."

"It's *fine*," I snapped because it really wasn't but I

didn't have the wherewithal to say anything else. "Let's find what I need and get out of here."

"We're not staying the night?" She didn't have the right to sound so disappointed, in my opinion. I had to remind myself that she was still new to this, still green, and that her obvious arrogant shift came from the success of an adventure that was feeding this side of her I didn't like.

Been there, or, at least, been around that. Campaign confidence was one of the things I hated about being in adventure groups. Honestly, I never thought Fig would fall prey to it, had been pretending whatever was going on with her wasn't that. But it was clear now that I'd simply been deceiving myself and that my old and dear Fig Marigold was caught in the clutches of the dreaded bane that was the worst thing that could happen to a new adventurer. Yes, death was the second. Trust me, this was worse because guess what it often led to? While many newbies died in their first campaigns, more than that perished due to stupid, unrelenting confidence in their second.

Call it fear for her future that had me furious and leave it at that, shall we?

## CHAPTER THREE

Whatever the truth of the matter, whether anxiety for her or embarrassment and frustration for me, I spun away from her and rode on, careful to keep my head down and my hands on the reins, letting Pennywhistle pick his way through the crowd on the street. I wasn't really watching where I was going at first. I just needed time to uncoil and shed my temper and my horse was my best indicator. His shift would alert me when I'd done enough. I could feel his tail slapping my leg, caught his twitching against the bit, the way his ears laid back more than they perked forward. When he finally settled I had, too, the pair of us pausing, as luck would have it, outside a tavern and inn combo, but not on purpose.

Not that Fig realized it. "Perfect," she said brightly,

like nothing had happened. "They'll be needing a bard, no doubt."

"I doubt it," I grumbled. "Cities like this are usually more than able to maintain a full complement of bards that perform in circuit. I won't be welcome to stay." I wasn't interested in local politics and honestly, most bards were jerks, present company excepted (most of the time). Their continual jockeying for position, prestige and attention made my stomach churn and, I think, was part of the reason my mentor, Simon Lyric, had accepted me. The Royal Bard had only taken three apprentices in his career and while I worried at times the only reason he'd chosen me was due to his connection to my parents, Simon himself never tried to be noticed or sought out recognition. He was just the best and his brilliance simply elevated him of its own accord.

Of course, it helped that Mom and Dad had the trust and ear of both monarchs and that Simon had first been heard by them thanks to my parents. Still, I had no doubt the old elf's charm and talent would have landed him as the head of his guild and a member of the Guild itself eventually.

My mentor and I agreed on one thing. Bring music and message to the people who didn't get to hear it nearly enough and a bard would never, ever want for an audience. A place like this, however? I wrinkled my nose as I looked around. Trying this place would mean a fight for ears, coins and focus, all drawing the kind of attention I really didn't want. Incognito as a Yestervere daughter hiding out in plain sight only worked when I wasn't anywhere I could be recognized.

Pennywhistle pawed the ground, the grinding sound I'd been unhappily contemplating from his right front shoe giving me pause. While it might last a bit longer, I knew he was in dire need of a quality farrier and blacksmith and my guitar new strings. Not to mention a refill on certain spices and my favorite tea mixture I wasn't even sure if they'd stock here in Vorentine.

Still, maybe we should move on. There was a village I knew of just a day's ride further along the border, after all, of a smaller size with less likelihood for trouble.

Except, of course, Pennywhistle's pawing was simply the Fates playing tricks, because just as I considered the possibility, wouldn't you know two nails came loose and the whole stupid shoe rolled free down the street?

"Fine," I grumbled to him as I stepped down from the saddle, soothing him with my touch if not my tone. "We'll stay." Just as long as it took to sort him out.

Fig was already tossing Twinkletoes' reins in my direction, dashing into the inn and tavern, while I ordered my horse to stand, the pony's control over his pommel, before going after the traitor curve of iron. By the time I returned—dodging a trotting mare and two large carriages in the process—Fig was retreating from the doorway, face bright red and anger back on the surface.

A burly man in a white apron, his bald head

tattooed with elaborate swirls and lines, glared at me with his fists on his hips. "Bards," he snorted. "I've got more bards coming to my place than I can beat off with a stick." That sounded like a threat.

"Then I advise you to buy another stick," I said rather pertly, despite myself, "and save yourself some effort next time." I led Pennywhistle away, not willing to ride him as he limped on uneven hooves down the street.

Fig did the same, strutting like a young cock about to crow. "He has no idea who he just turned away," she said.

"Nor will he ever find out," I said. "Honestly, Fig. We need to talk about this."

She cringed, deflating. "I don't know what's gotten into me," she said. "You're right. We should just go."

"Not going to happen until I find someone to take care of poor Pennywhistle," I said. "Come on, Fig. Let's find a more suitable part of the city where maybe the likes of us might find a place that fits."

She perked and nodded, and though I relented and tried to shift my own attitude, we were still going to have that talk.

We'd ended up in a rather expensive part of the city and while I was hardly a slouch in the performance department, I preferred something a little less competitive. That meant as we circled toward the outer edge of the city again, down closer to where the markets filled the air with the scent of delicious foods, it was clear we'd exited the edge of one price point and found something more to my liking.

The inn I chose carefully, spotting it down the street and keeping an eye on it as we approached. The exterior was in need of a paint job but the structure looked sound and someone had recently updated the sign hanging out front. When I peeked in the windows from across the way, the taproom didn't appear overly full, but nor was it empty and when I left Fig with the horses to drift over and lean against the wall, I caught a heady whiff of deliciousness that meant whoever owned this place knew how to cook.

Or their staff did. And that was an excellent sign indeed.

"Stay," I mouthed at Fig, pointing at her while she visibly argued with me, though silently. I didn't wait for her to yell, turning and going inside. My elf vision quickly adapted to the dim light, and I liked what I saw, the low benches lining the walls pushed back for now but grooves in the uneven stone floor making it obvious that the corner stage area was used for shows in the past. The furniture looked heavy and a bit rough but well-maintained, the bar a solid centerpiece, the customers digging into their food and drink with relish. As for the woman behind the counter, she smiled when I approached.

"Bright afternoon, Good Lady," I said. "While I know it's a stretch, would you be in need of a bard of some skill this evening?" I asked with a smile and a self-deprecating tone.

To my surprise, she perked. "As a matter of fact," she said. "We don't get a lot of songsmiths down here, truth be told. Soama Purvelo," she offered her hand which I gripped at the wrist.

"Elora Tune," I said, letting her go to sweep her a little bow. "Good Lady Purvello."

She blushed and touched her dark hair, wound tight into two matching buns on the sides of her head, her round cheeks pink. It was clear she wasn't used to being talked to that way, more's the pity. "I'm no lady," she said. "But you're welcome here at the Thistledown, Bard Tune, if you'd like to play." She hesitated a moment before nodding. "I'll have you aware, though, our place is independent of the merchant masters, which means you may not gain the kind of audience you're used to."

Interesting and not a problem at all. Playing at a place unbeholden to one merchant house or another didn't trouble me in the least and meant I'd chosen well. "Perfect," I said, leaning in to wink at her. "I prefer to pair my entrepreneurial bent to that of those of a similar mind."

She seemed happy about that, too. Which meant one thing was actually going to go right. Then again, I worried as I negotiated the deal and then returned outside to fetch Fig, there was a reason no one chose this place for their shows.

Too late now and honestly, how much worse could my day get?

Fates, Elora. Why did I always have to tempt the Fates?

Because the moment I stepped out into the street, focused on Fig and the question in my mind, I realized my mistake. Saw it in her wide, terrified stare, in her slow-motion wave and how her mouth opened to yell my name.

Too late. I was already in the path of the big, black carriage barreling toward me.

And there was no way I'd get out of its path in time.

Bard pancake anyone?

## CHAPTER FOUR

The thing about being an elf? Cat-like reflexes that meant I made an instantaneous reaction, leaping forward in the nick of time and rolling to a successful save out of the thundering hooves and their oncoming threat.

Ahem. That is. I mean...

Um, hm. I tripped. Fine, all right? I admit it. In that exact moment when even my incredible reaction time wasn't going to be enough, the Fates stepped in again (laughing at me, no doubt) and did to me what they'd done to my horse.

The toe seam of my boot let go. Which caught on the cobblestone and sent me sprawling. A sprawl, I will tell you, I managed to turn into a graceful dodge and tuck, so I'm sure it looked intentional. Right, sure it did. Regardless of appearances, instead of being crushed under eight (make that sixteen) very heavy hooves of the four giant black horses pulling the impressively massive carriage that almost took me out, I instead survived to sing another day.

I'd take it.

As I sprang to my feet next to Fig, just grateful to be alive, she grasped for me, gaping and her mouth flapping before she hugged me so hard that I was sure she bruised a rib.

Or did that happen when I fell headlong into the street? Whatever the case, I gently extracted her and shook my head at her trickle of tears, positive that despite my calm in the moment that I'd be blubbering myself as soon as I had a second to process and find a quiet corner to let my terror out.

For now, it would have to sit inside me like a fluttering pixie.

"Are you okay?" My friend checked me over while I nodded, exhaling the breath that should have been crushed from my chest. She glared down the street at the passing carriage even as I noted that same crest as I'd seen on the guard, the one on the gate. Whoever was in that very large conveyance was either a Vorentine or closely associated to them.

Even more reason to want to leave this wretched place behind.

I hated cities so much.

I did note that the carriage came to an abrupt halt just a few doors down and, as those forced to go around it ducked and curtsied or bowed—not royal, huh? Close enough—I did see a tall woman in a huge, black gown step down from it and go inside a local establishment. She wasn't alone, either, a more flamboyantly dressed woman on her heels, in bright yellow and pink, the sickening clash of the two colors doing nothing for her pale complexion and dyed blonde hair. She looked around with a smile that felt acquisitive to me.

A third woman trailed behind them both, head down, her matron's uniform that of a servant. She stopped beside the back of the carriage to wait for her mistress(es?), hands clasped in front of her.

But it was the interesting young man who oozed around the corner to glare at the carriage who had my attention the most. I think the only reason I noticed him was because I was so hyper focused thanks to my near-collision with the carriage in question. And, to be fair, though he might have passed inspection by others less accustomed to his kind, it was obvious to me that he was either in the beginnings of rogue training or had learned sufficient skills from someone of that calling to make himself obvious.

For some reason, rogue skills always got worse before they got better. If the trainees in question lasted long enough, that was.

He didn't see me notice him, too intent on his target for that, a sure sign of lack of training. Nor did I spot a Guild badge (or any sign) denoting his status. Which meant he was likely a common thief scouting a score. Well, it wouldn't go down the way he thought if he got caught, which he would, acting all sneaky and skulking like that. Then again, this wasn't a Guild city, so he wouldn't be chastised by his mentor the way I might expect. Or then again, perhaps he'd fare worse. Freeholds had their own rules and I wasn't attuned to the ones that made Vorentine tick.

Nor did I want to sort that particular set of standards out because that would mean trouble and I was planning to avoid anything to do with danger, mayhem or poking my nose in where it wasn't wanted if at all possible.

Then again, I did have Fig with me. Maybe brushing up on local laws might have been a smart choice after all.

My little gnome friend didn't seem to realize I'd shifted my attention and was still brushing at my clothes, muttering about taking care of me (imagine those tables turned!) when the woman in black exited into the street again and alighted the carriage. The colorful one followed, the matron waiting until they were both inside before stepping up.

Only to hesitate as she spotted the young man I was watching. They exchanged a most obvious look that had me shaking my head for them both and the melodrama that I really needed to stay far, far away from (because it was clear to me that whatever he was up to wasn't going to end well) when Fig tensed next to me and pointed.

"Hey," she said. "Isn't that Mellie?"

My whole being jerked, my gaze whipping away from the servant now behind the closed door as the carriage moved off again, the young man slouching as he retreated.

Right into a furious confrontation with none other than Guild Master Rogue Mellicant Savos.

# CHAPTER FIVE

It wasn't that I would have preferred not to interact with the Guild master rogue in question. I had no real reservations about reconnecting with her. While our first interaction wasn't always ideal, we'd parted ways on a positive note, at least as far as I was concerned.

On the other hand, it was clear to me that she had her own agenda to fulfill and, upon hearing Fig's voice, spun and stared us both down with a scowl that indicated she either hadn't anticipated being seen by anyone who knew who she was or, just as possibly, aimed that particular unhappiness at us specifically and with purpose.

Whatever her intention for the snap of her focus, it didn't last. Instead of approaching us, Mellie snatched the arm of the young man who'd been skulking around the carriage and physically dragged his sullen self around the corner and out of sight, down a side alley perfect for just that purpose.

"Are we going after her?" Fig looked up at me with her typical eagerness right there on the surface. "I smell an adventure."

Of course, she did. Which meant I had to fight very, very hard not to eye roll and sigh. I managed it, too, despite everything. "I'm sure if she has something to share with us, she'll make her presence known," I said. "But it's her business, Fig, not ours."

My gnome friend's nose-wrinkle said she believed otherwise, hardly a surprise. "I'm going to see what she's up to," she said. "Are you sure you're not in for a bit of poking around?"

I took Twinkletoes' reins from her again and shrugged. "Have fun," I said.

She flashed me a giant grin before dodging across the street, much more carefully than I had and without incident. I'd like to note that there were no giant and threatening carriages rumbling past at the time, so any sort of danger posed was mitigated in her case.

Just saying.

The cobblestone courtyard of the inn stood in the back, both mounts following me without complaint as I hobbled my way around. My flapping sole had me frustrated, though to be fair it only added to my previous irritation, never mind the fact that bit of annoyance had saved my life. The plain, burly man who greeted me, a heavy leather apron over his clothing, smiled regardless of my attitude, shaking my hand the same way the woman inside had.

"Soama told me you're staying the night and playing for us, Bard Tune," he said. "Welcome, welcome. I'm Hathin, her husband. She handles the inside and I the out, with good reason." He laughed at that, a hearty and kind sound, though he seemed anxious to please. "Can I stable your horses for you?"

"I find myself in need of a farrier," I said before looking down again at my boot. "And a cobbler."

He nodded immediately, taking Twinkletoes to a small pen and quickly divesting her of her tack. I watched him efficiently deal with the pony as her attempts to nip and stomp gained her only a soft pat and deft management. I accepted the key he offered me for the tack box he loaded with my friend's saddle, bridle and bags, adding mine to the mix while I exchanged Pennywhistle's headgear for a halter of soft rope.

"One street down and over," Hathin said as he quickly rubbed the pony down. She relented in her nasty attempts to bite him, leaning into his ministrations with groan. "As for Junna the Smith. She and her partner, Uni are the best in the area."

"I'll make sure to mention you," I said with a nod.

"As for a cobbler," he said, letting the pony free to much some hay while Pennywhistle sighed over the fact he wasn't joining her, "there's a few on that street might be suitable." He looked down at his own boots, the worn leather rough and clearly homemade. "Not much in the market for such things, I'm afraid."

"I'm sure I'll make do," I said. "With my thanks." I locked the tack box and led my gelding out again, strolling the street with my head down and my destination in mind. A steady hum of a soft tune kept my boot intact enough for the trip, but it was necessary to maintain the song under my breath the whole time, an irritating fact that distracted me. Not that I needed all of my wits about me, but this wasn't the best part of the city. Then again, it was far from the worst, either. Still, I knew better than to let my guard down, not taking chances on being confronted with further conflict, including making myself a target for pickpockets.

Which naturally had me worrying about my friend while I firmly set that worry aside (several times, in fact, over the course of the walk as it kept rising again despite my choice) and reminded myself that she was a grown gnome. No, she wasn't very experienced yet and I still feared deep in the throws of confidence unearned, but I'd agreed to allow her the space to figure things out on her own long before today.

It did make me a little sad as I turned the corner and headed for the end of the street and the large smithy there. The more she learned and explored and adventured, the more likely it was that our paths would part for good. Hopefully not due to the fate that took so many, though, Fates be kind. She'd outgrow me as long as she kept her wits about her and survived.

Just a truth that wasn't the end of the world but still tweaked my emotions, even after the frustration she'd put me through. In the end, regardless of her attitude or her lack of wisdom, Fig was my friend.

The young man who greeted me quickly connected me with a big half-orc woman whose lower tusks had been polished to a bright lavender that matched her eyes.

"Nice of Hathin to send you," she said in a surprising soprano, one massive hand giving Pennywhistle a gentle pat. She gestured toward the yard and the short, burly dwarf woman, her shaved head shining in the sunlight as much as her deep, amber beard, who was ministering to the hooves of a large draft horse. "We'll put you on the list. An hour?"

The time and price negotiated—four new shoes recommended and bound to put a dent in my money pouch, so be it—I left my horse in their competent care and crossed to the next corner, already having spotted the sign for a cobbler's and now in desperate need as the entire flap of my boot's sole had come free in my hand.

The front door chimed, a small set of bells over the threshold announcing my entry into the dim and quiet space. The mixed scent of leather, dye and the slightly sweet hit of pixie dust had me smiling because I knew I'd made a good choice. I loved seeing that adorable race at work, their production always top-notch, and noted as the small man—likely half-gnome himself from his diminutive stature—who hurried toward me from the back of the store smiled kindly at the pair of fluttering workers who waved to me over their tasks.

"Welcome, welcome," he said. "Leeth Lacebow, at

your service. Ah, you're in special need!" He pointed at the leather in my hand and then at my foot. "Thrix, Rox!" The two pixies rushed toward us in a sparkle of wings and dust, their smiles as sweet as the increased sugar scent their presence added to the air. "A repair, my dear?"

I grimaced down at my boots, the pixies giggling at my exaggerated expression, made just for them. "I fear these have seen the end of the roads they've taken me on." I'd already decided to replace them, two full years of riding having worn the sides to a thinness that barely protected me from chafing any longer, the soles barely thick enough to shield from stones. The fact that the boot that fell apart on me just now hadn't done so weeks ago was only thanks to a whisper of magic that held it together. "I'm in need of new, I think."

"Of course," Leeth said, nodding sagely. "Fitted or precut for you, good traveler?"

The price of precut was, naturally, a great deal less but knowing I had pixies at hand? "Let's do fitted," I said, trying not to groan inwardly. My poor savings were taking a hit today. Honestly, I was just being ridiculous and could certainly afford the expense. But all this time on the road had made me a bit of a tightwad.

Still, if I had learned one thing about this life I'd chosen, quality meant the difference between something lasting or failing at a critical moment.

The pixies went right to work, leading me into the shop and seating me on a stool, their rapid-fire conversation tinkling with music in their lovely, lilting language. I was the only customer for the moment, so I took advantage of the opportunity to speak to Leeth, especially after noting the familiar crest that he displayed at the front of his counter.

"You're affiliated with the Vorentine merchant family," I said.

He nodded instantly, though the joy seemed to go out of him, if only for a moment. "Indeed," he said, observing the pixies at their work but not interfering. "Our ruling family," Leeth added with a nod.

Like that wasn't obvious. Rather than push him, I changed the subject.

"Nice to see you employing such talent," I said, both of the small and sparkly folk pausing to giggle at me before going back to work. Their small hands tickled as they created their magical pattern, efficient and enthusiastic, touch light.

"Thrix and Rox have been with me for ten years now," he beamed at them. "The best staff I could ask for."

They chattered at him happily in their own language before going back to work.

His attitude had me relaxing further. It had only been thirty years since pixies had been removed from the "monster" roster and deemed citizens of Valoria. Up until then, it had been perfectly legal to enslave them, something easy to do since pixies were notoriously innocent and malleable, their size—barely half that of gnomes—making them easy targets for poachers.

As impossible as it was to tell their gender, I guessed the blue-toned one as a male who left the pinkish one suddenly, my old boots in his magical grasp, floating them toward a workbench while his partner zipped away with the pattern glowing beside her for my fresh set. I hadn't had a great deal of opportunity to watch pixies at work, though I was familiar enough with the basics of their magic.

"Thrix will have your boot repaired and ready for you in short order," Leeth told me. "It will take Rox until morning to complete your new ones. I hope that timing is convenient?"

"Considering a regular cobbler would take longer," I laughed, "that works for me."

He flashed me a smile, thick, blunt teeth very white, pointed ears of his gnome heritage showing through his carefully styled dark hair confirming my guess. "They really are remarkable," he said, "though I do love taking on a special order or two."

And I'd just insulted the man, whoops. "It must be nice to be able to spend your time working on such things," I said, "and leaving the day-to-day to them."

"Indeed," he said. "And certainly increases my opportunity for customers."

"Which makes your merchant family happy," I said with a smile.

Again with that flicker of anxiety that he hid behind his answering nod. "Of course," Leeth said.

"Tell me, has the Vorentine merchant line always governed here?" Freehold cities often changed names and hands with the rise and fall of family dominance, unlike royal towns and villages that remained in the control of the ruling bloodlines whose territories they were built in.

"We've been blessed to bear the Vorentine name for the last twenty years," he said like he meant it, even if his eyes said otherwise. "Though we recently lost the patriarch of the house." Leeth was doing a very good job pretending to be sorrowful. None of what he said reached his expressive gaze, which told me way more than his words ever would. Exactly his intent, perhaps? "The loss of Balmont Vorentine is still felt, though we're fortunate that his wife Theringale was already such a driving force behind the success of their operations."

In other words, the old boss was a total and utter tyrant and his wife was just as bad, if not worse. Got it.

"It's my first visit to Vorentine in a decade," I said, distantly aware of an approaching rumble that felt familiar, my elf and bard senses attuned to sound even when I didn't try. "The city seems even more prosperous and well-maintained for a location so near the Everwilding border." Something rumbled to a halt outside and I caught myself shifting my focus toward the door.

Leeth hadn't noticed, perhaps because this time his full expression suggested he agreed with me. "Say what you will," he told me, dropping his tone just a little, "but we are well protected. Even if we pay for it." His grimace smoothed instantly as the doorbell chimed, the entry flashing light into the dim space as someone entered.

A figure who didn't surprise me because I had anticipated her appearance thanks to the behemoth approach of her giant carriage.

Leeth turned with that same professional smile I'd been greeted with, no hint of his real feelings exposed. And, to his credit, he didn't falter 'even a little when the door thudded shut, no longer silhouetting the looming woman who'd entered.

Not that it mattered. Draped fully in black, from her massive dress to the lace over her long, dark hair, the woman from the carriage that almost ran me down might as well have shut out the sun with the scowl on her face instead of the door she'd let close behind her.

Let me guess. Theringale Vorentine.

How dramatic.

# CHAPTER SIX

She wasn't alone long, the door opening again, the loudly dressed woman who'd accompanied her earlier stepping through like she was the Vorentine and I wondered if I'd somehow gotten the wrong vibe. Except Leeth was already sweeping toward the taller of the two, bowing to her despite the fact she wasn't nobility. "Madam Vorentine," he said in a voice that rang with respect. "Welcome."

She snapped her fingers, the woman beside her handing her a sheet of parchment absently, already perusing the offerings in the shop. I noted her acquisitive smirk as she fingered an expensive-looking pair of gold booties while the towering mistress of the merchant family perused the page a moment.

"Leeth Lacebow," she said in a dull, unfriendly

tone. "Cobbler."

"How lovely to welcome you back to my establishment," he said, clearly having gone through this before. The fact that she'd made no effort to remember him wasn't endearing her to me, though it was fair enough that if she made the rounds as she appeared to be doing, she had a lot of people on her list. Still, make an effort, I say.

"Your rent is due," she said in that same empty, flat voice while her companion continued to peruse the merchandise.

"Ooh, Theringale," the pink and yellow gowned blonde whose ringlet curls really better suited a young woman, not a matron of her age, "I simply *must* have these slippers."

The widow Vorentine glanced her way, expression locked and stony. "Wrap them," she said without looking at Leeth.

His instant of hesitation melted into a soft rounding of his shoulders and I recognized defeat when I saw it. "Of course, ma'am," he said, fetching the gold leather slippers, retreating behind the counter to do her bidding.

It wasn't until Theringale snapped again that I noted the matronly servant had joined her, that quiet soul stepping forward to accept a small metal box from Leeth which she turned and handed to her mistress.

Tall, dark and spooky weighed the offering in one palm, frown tightening. "You're short," she said. She could tell by feel? Impressive and more than a little unnerving.

"My apologies, Madam Vorentine," he said, faint tremble in his voice, hands shaking as he wrapped up the slippers. "It's been a bit slow this fortnight."

Whether she believed him—or empathized—or not, I was now battling my opinion of the widowed merchant boss. First, the fact that she personally saw to her own business was the kind of attention to detail that one didn't often see from someone of her stature. Why not send staff to do so? Second, her entire attitude left so much to be desired it was no wonder Leeth's response to any questions about her and her name were met with outward positivity and inward restraint.

"Theringale," her flowery companion said with a rather evil innocence that suggested she had a purpose to her interruption, "aren't you getting tired of hearing such complaints? Here you are taking the time to do your once-a-year tour and not a single merchant has said even a thank you Madam Vorentine for all your hard work on their behalf. Only whined about custom and their failure at business."

Ah, so this was an annual roundup then, that made sense.

"Indeed, Yarra," Theringale said, faint frown the only indication that she was human and not some towering black-clad statue with a voice. "While my friend, Madam Astir, is not a businesswoman, even she understands the gravity of this situation, cobbler. Most displeasing."

"I assure you," Leeth rushed to say, "I've been

working hard to increase my business." He glanced my way, panic on his face, and I instantly wanted to rescue him. But he wasn't done spluttering and apologizing. "I'm certain this next quarter will be far more profitable."

"Maybe if you didn't hire pixies," Yarra Astir sneered, "you'd be able to afford to pay your mistress what she's owed."

"Enough," Theringale said, her companion simpering but falling silent at the steady command. "According to my tallies," she looked at the sheet of parchment again, "this is the third time you've failed to reach quota."

Leeth wiped at his upper lip but didn't argue. While, to my surprise, I noted the serving woman, now holding the box with the slippers, glared sideways at her mistress in what looked to me to be pure derision.

Her eyes then met mine and, with a flash of fear, dropped to the floor, face composed again.

Interesting. And none of my business.

As much as I wished otherwise, this wasn't my fight. And not that I was excusing Theringale Vorentine, she had the right to set whatever rules she saw fit, just like Leeth had the right to leave and go elsewhere. Besides, I'd seen nobility act far worse toward those who called their towns home.

Didn't make it right, no. I just had to live in this world, not love everything about it. Mind you, there was one thing I could do, and fully intended to, as was a bard's prerogative. As I sat there and observed in silence, seething on the inside and introspective on the out, I was already secretly planning a scathing and cutting song that I'd make sure to perform as soon as it was done.

"You have one fortnight to cover the rent in arrears," Theringale said, turning without another word and exiting.

Leeth's muttered compliance was met with a jaunty finger wave from Yarra, who snatched her unpaid prize from the hands of the serving woman before following the widow Vorentine out into the street. I noted that the matron cast a sympathetic look at the cobbler before exiting, the door thudding shut behind them all, leaving the dim interior of the shop deathly quiet.

Only then did I realize, as tinkling sounded behind me, that the pixies had gone into hiding, only emerging again now that the coast was clear, peeking out and floating back to their work benches with anxious expressions.

Now I really *was* concerned. "That was intense," I said to Leeth who spun toward me, trying to school his face into cheery confidence and failing as his quivering lips gave his lingering anxiety away.

"Madam Vorentine is a force of nature," he agreed, sagging against the counter.

"I'm sorry to hear things are hard for you," I said.

"For everyone," he nodded. Leeth hesitated before shrugging like he'd made a decision he hadn't planned on. "The truth is, our city has never been more on edge or in such dire financial straits." His little hands wrung as the pixies chattered sadly at him. "When

Master Vorentine passed, everything changed." He shook his head, now visibly sorrowful himself. "Balmont wasn't a great master by any means, but he knew when to ease up on the businesses who looked to him. His wife doesn't share that subtly."

Bleeding them dry while demanding they hand over valuable products without payment for her little friend certainly wasn't helping. "Sounds like someone has royal aspirations," I said.

Leeth flinched, his eyes tightening around the edges. "Or likes to act as though she has that power," he said. Then inhaled a sharp breath. "Oh my, forgive me." He waved off my attempt to continue the conversation. "Here I am busy gossiping and your boots are repaired." He took the damaged footwear from the blue-toned pixie and examined it briefly before nodding in satisfaction. "This will tide you over until your new ones are ready. We'll see you in the morning?" The pinkish pixie chimed in agreement, her partner bowing to me in mid-air before flying off to help her.

I paid him for the completed repair, leaving a hefty tip and extra for each pixie while he tried to deny my offer.

"I appreciate good work," I said, not even wincing this time as I tucked my purse away. "I'll see you shortly."

The sun had set past the line of taller buildings in the West by the time I emerged, turning toward the smithy and farrier yard to check in on my horse. As it happened, the carriage hadn't rolled off on its rumbling way just yet, Madam Vorentine emerging from yet another storefront, this one looking like a seamstress shop, her companion Yarra Astir again toting an item that I was willing to bet she hadn't compensated the owner for.

That wasn't what interested me, however. Instead, it was the return of the skulking young man from earlier, the same one that Mellie had led away, who caught my attention and held it. I paused to adjust my boot to keep from being so obvious about my interest, though he didn't seem to notice I was watching. Utterly amateur and if Mellie was some sort of mentor to him, I judged her for the terrible job she'd done in his basic training.

None of which mattered, ultimately. The Vorentine party returned to the interior of the carriage and rolled off in the same loud and obnoxious manner, the young man waiting until they'd begun their ride to go after them.

I didn't see Fig anywhere about and could only hope that she'd lost track of both Mellie and the young man. Which had me still feeling uncomfortable as I turned and walked the other way in a deliberate stride, repaired boot holding up with magic and a prayer, off to mind my own freaking business.

Mostly.

*Take every cent and don't leave a copper,*
*Wring them dry, it's only proper.*
*Who would they be without our protection?*
*Rent and gifts the price from their limited selection.*

*Take every cent!*

At the rate the song was writing itself, I might or might not have been ready to try it out that very night.

## CHAPTER SEVEN

I found myself with a much lighter purse as I led Pennywhistle back toward the inn, though the satisfying ring of his new shoes on the cobblestones— metal reinforced with dwarf magic, no less— comforted me in knowing that he'd been well cared for and was now prepared for many more miles on the road.

"You went above and beyond," I'd told the amber-bearded Uni who just grunted in reply before leaving me to get back to work, her partner grinning in apology.

"She's better with horses," the half-orc had said in her lovely soprano. "We appreciate your business. Tell Hathin and Soama we'll be by tonight for a pint and to hear you play."

I'd grinned and nodded, though when Junna's eyebrows rose at the extra coin I dropped in her palm, I'd just shrugged. "Trust me, the miles Pennywhistle carries me, I value good work and the time and magic put into his safekeeping." Truth, all of it. Besides, I had more money stashed in the lockbox hidden away in the secret place Mom had spelled for that purpose, her gift for the road that I'd put to good use all these years. Being a skinflint when it wasn't necessary wasn't a good look for me. And if I could help local artisans and tradespeople who really did deserve it, I would choose to every time. "I'll be spreading the word with everyone I know looking for the same."

She grimaced just a little. "I hope you'll accept a beer on us," she said. "The word of a bard goes long and deep and truth be told, custom has been tough of late." She clamped her lips tight, tusks leaving imprints in her skin from her tension. "Sorry, no complaints. We're lucky to have such protections in such a great city this close to the border. See you at the Thistledown, Bard Tune!" She spun and strode away from me, leaving me to frown and seek out something I hadn't bothered to look for prior to that.

And only noted the emblem of the Vorentine family over their gate because I was now paying attention.

During that walk back to the inn I took the long way around, winding my way through a few streets and checking in on many of the storefronts. While there were a handful of other merchant markings about, most of them were either paired with (dominated by) the Vorentine one in cooperation or very small and scattered, their business owners nervous and their places appearing in need of attention.

When I finally returned to the inn, I was reminded why it was that Soama and Hathin seemed grateful I was willing to play for them because you better believe I went looking for the Vorentine hallmark. And didn't find it anywhere. Of course not. They were independent. She'd already told me as much. Being such in a freehold city wasn't exactly dangerous, but it did take courage because lack of association with other businesses who banded together to support each other was distinctly absent. Not to mention the fact they'd be the last to be protected in case of disaster, like fire or attacks from the Everwilding, on their own when it came to theft, brigands or general damage from unhappy customers. The couple rose in my estimation further for their desire to stand alone, and when I handed the reins over to Hathin, Pennywhistle happily nuzzling his little dappled friend, I shook the man's hand.

"I previously agreed to play a set," I said. "I'm going to do three. And you're not to pay me. I'll take what I get in tips and call it square."

He spluttered, Soama emerging from the back door, wiping her hands on her apron at that very moment. She'd clearly caught what I'd said because she joined us in a rush, shaking her head, but I crossed my arms over my chest and grinned.

"Take the deal or not," I said.

They exchanged a look and yes, I caught the relief

on Soama's face even if Hathin looked embarrassed.

"We'll take it," she said, "if you'll stay and eat for free."

"You're lucky I'm not much of a drinker or eater," I said with a laugh, shaking both of their hands to seal the deal. "Now, if you don't mind, I'd like to freshen up and get settled before nightfall."

The room was small but very clean, the linens not new but crisply fresh and someone had lovingly pieced together the patchwork quilts that warmed the two small single beds.

"You let me know if you're needing a single thing," Soama said from the doorway, hesitating, cheeks pink. "We're most grateful to you for choosing us, Bard Tune."

"I'm happy to do it," I said. "I'm independent myself for a reason."

She bobbed a nod, acknowledging what I implied without saying so. "Privy's at the back and you've access to a bathhouse if needed. I'll leave you to prepare." Her gaze slid lovingly over my guitar case, my saddlebags now piled on the floor alongside Fig's who had yet to return. "I do love music," she murmured in a hopeful voice.

Then music she would have.

First things first, however. I needed guitar strings and to find my tea. While wishing the pixies had worked a bit faster. As fine a patch job as Thrix had done in holding my old one together, I could feel my foot fighting against the magic that supported the weakened sole. Morning for new, custom boots was magically fast, but my feet disagreed.

My stroll back into the city came with the final part of the plan, making it easier to explore without Pennywhistle at my side. I covered multiple streets and sections of the city, overhearing more than a few mutters in the process of seeking out the instrument shop and the herbalist, all suggesting that not only did the Vorentine widow own the majority of the properties in this area, her rents had gone up since her husband's passing half a year ago and she'd been using the proceeds to buy up more of the city from her competitors.

I knew from experience what came next, frowning at the toe of my damaged boot as I crossed the street back past the inn, three sets of new strings and a pouch of tea tucked away inside my jerkin. My comment to Leeth Lacebow earlier about royalty hadn't been fully in jest. While I didn't agree with it, there were those who would sell their titles to commoners for large sums of money. It might have been frowned upon, but as long as no one died—and the titles were relatively minor ones—the king and queen didn't usually do much to curtail such activity.

In fact, Mom mentioned once that the monarchs thought such activity injected new life and ambition into the ruling class. I wasn't so sure they were right—or that my mother's stoic delivery meant she agreed—but I wasn't in the know or in any position to fight them on it.

What I was certain of? Whether her people knew or not, it was now obvious to me that Theringale

Vorentine was positioning herself to buy a title and become a real Lady.

The question was, whose title was she buying? And was this her idea alone or had her husband been part of the plot?

Whatever the case, it didn't matter, did it? Not when I was forced to come to an abrupt halt when I realized none other than the massive black carriage stood outside Soama and Hathin's inn and tavern, the Thistledown. Why was she there? They weren't beholden to her. Was she bullying them? Worry turned to amusement as, in a flurry and a public show of humiliation, the tall and imposing widow Vorentine firmly dragged someone from the taproom and tried to escort him to the cabin of her carriage.

Only to have the same young man who'd allowed me passage into this very city to jerk free of her, spinning and almost falling as he did, drunker than ever as he faced her.

"Leave me be, Mother," he said, just decipherable past the effects of drink.

"Justes," she snarled, her blank and empty coldness replaced by icy fury, "get in the carriage."

"I won't," he huffed at her, arms rising and falling in a flopping motion that reminded me of a gangly stork trying to rise from a riverside. And failing. "And you can't make me."

A less-than-regal argument ending in a drunken standoff in a public street, was it? I might have preferred otherwise at other times, but I was still a bard and there was nothing like first-hand observation of family interactions.

Hey, a job is a job. And yes, especially in this case, since I was already halfway through a song about just this particular bloodline.

Vibrating with rage, she stared him down while everyone else on the street stopped to watch. To whisper. While she fumed and visibly hesitated over what came next.

My, my. How entertaining.

# CHAPTER EIGHT

There was zero doubt in my mind that Theringale Vorentine was acutely aware of the fact that her son was making a massive idiot of himself in front of everyone on the street. And that she was contemplating murdering him in full view just to end the humiliation.

Part of me sympathized, despite myself. It couldn't be easy to run a vast network of business interests, especially widowed and struggling to pull all of the threads she no doubt had to in order to ensure her success continued. While I didn't personally feel ambition, I did understand it. And while I disagreed with her practices and her now clear intent to dominate her city and become a noblewoman, there was no question that she'd done what she'd set out to do with sheer determination while keeping her city safe under the kind of circumstances that often warranted calling in the Guild or the Guard.

So, that being said, I also understood her son's perspective. As the youngest of the Yestervere family with an epic parental unit and two highly decorated and gloriously celebrated siblings, my own choice to not pursue adventure and accolades meant I'd stepped out of the limelight on purpose. That didn't mean I couldn't sympathize with what the weight of all that glittery, glowy, gargantuan pressure meant. I'd seen more than enough children of the famous and royal turn to vices of various kinds to smother their feelings of inadequacy. I'd like to think that I was above such choices but honestly? If it hadn't been for my mentor and the fact that I had music, I don't know how things would have ended up for me.

But there was a huge difference between understanding with empathy and forgiving unnecessarily harsh and inhuman behavior. All it took was one glance sideways at the doorway to the taproom where Soama and Hathin stood in anxious observation for my compassion's targeting to switch immediately from those who had to those who only wanted to live in peace while providing a service.

You know who I picked to side with. If there was any doubt, you still have a lot to learn about me. Stick around. Education to come.

The yellow and pink flouncing companion of the darkly angry widow chose right then to alight from the carriage, her tight and eager nastiness focused on young Justes.

"You really shouldn't talk back to your mother," Yarra Astir said.

"Shut up, Yarra," he bit back at her with a grimace.

"Are you going to let him continue to humiliate you, my dear Theringale?" Yarra's fake shock hid nothing and I doubted the widowed businesswoman took her fraudulent concern at face value.

For whatever reason, however, Theringale chose not to correct the other woman, focusing instead on her son. Even as another carriage—this one smaller and painted blue—clattered into the street behind a pair of anxious horses, a young woman bursting out from the interior and rushing toward Justes.

"Darling," she said, reaching for him. He tried to shake her off while she clutched at his arm.

"About time you arrived, Darmilla," Yarra said with that same evil intent. Clearly, she was an instigator in this family's troubles, and I wondered why someone as smart and focused as Theringale allowed her to do so. "Honestly, your husband's behavior reflects badly on you. Surely, he'd be home and sober far more often if you'd just give the poor boy an heir or two."

Darmilla's cheeks burned but she didn't spare the nasty woman a glance. No, but Theringale did and for the first time I saw the widow Vorentine react to the horrible woman in yellow and pink.

She didn't say anything. She didn't have to. Yarra took one look and squeaked a little before ducking back into the black carriage and vanishing. Only then did I realize that the matron—Theringale's serving woman—was standing by the wheel and actively glared after the retreating Yarra.

I was very glad that my family got along as well as we did because if this was the sort of thing that Justes had to deal with on the daily? No wonder the poor kid was drunk.

"Deal with your husband, Darmilla," Theringale snapped. "I expect better from both of you." She swept toward her carriage, pausing to turn and confront the innkeeper couple. "If I catch you serving my son again," she said, "you'll no longer be welcome in Vorentine." She then climbed inside, her serving woman joining her without a word. The whole rig rumbled off almost before the door had closed, leaving the attractive young woman to glare her hate at its departure.

While Justes bent and, with a tidy kind of dignity that I hadn't expected, threw up on the hem of her dress.

Yikes. I was about to abandon him and his now horrified bride, the blonde girl in the lovely red dress stunned and embarrassed, when a silver-haired man rode up, sweeping down to the street from the large, black horse, expensive clothing in the same family velvet. He took one look and then spun in a slow circle, the watching crowd quickly stiffening, whispers going silent as he spoke in a loud and commanding voice.

"By order of the Vorentine Merchant family," he boomed, "you are ordered to disperse immediately or face the consequences."

When I say everyone bolted, I mean everyone. Even my new friends who ran the Thistledown vanished inside and firmly closed the door. Maybe I should have taken their lead, but I was honestly caught up in the drama and held my ground as the big, older man closed the distance to Justes and his young wife.

"Get him home," I heard the elder say.

"This isn't my fault, Racheff," Darmilla snapped at him.

"I know," he said. "But my sister won't see it that way. Please, my dear. Here, let me help you." He half-carried, half-guided Justes toward the carriage and inside.

"I don't want to go home, uncle," Justes said.

"Time to sleep off some of that drink, my boy," Racheff said, stepping back from the carriage as Darmilla joined her husband. I caught her disgust as Justes sagged next to her, but the uncle was already gesturing to the carriage driver. "Take them home."

And then he, too, retreated, swinging elegantly and gracefully back into his saddle before riding away. While his sister was clearly a businesswoman of great skill and his nephew an inebriated sop, the big man himself had spent time in the military or in a company of some kind.

I knew an old adventurer when I saw one.

The street had emptied all but for one person who really shouldn't have made himself so obvious, though I suppose he didn't know I had tagged his presence. Another mark against the young man who'd been following the black carriage, no Mellie in sight.

He wasn't my problem. In fact, Fig was looking for him as far as I knew and, if the master rogue's presence meant anything, Mellie was doing her best to keep this young thief in hand. Both of whom were failing, as far as I could see.

So, when he turned and headed toward the direction the black carriage had gone, I followed.

I swear it was instinct and not intentional. In fact, I'd barely made it to the other side of the street when I flinched and kicked myself internally. What was I doing? I had to go back to the Thistledown. Carry on with my own interests. I had a show to prepare for. Let the idiot youngster get himself in trouble. He wasn't mine to protect.

But I didn't get to spin and retreat. The moment I paused, someone reached out of the shadows between the two buildings where he'd first appeared and grabbed me. I was so surprised (and honestly ashamed of myself for missing the inevitable) that I staggered into the alley before I could stop my momentum.

Not surprised, however, to come face-to-face with a beautiful brunette who glared back at me like I was the one in trouble.

"Hello, Mellie," I said. "Lose someone who belonged to you?"

## CHAPTER NINE

"What are you doing here?" She hissed that in my face like I was following her or something.

"I seem to recall that *you* grabbed *me*," I said.

She only then appeared to realize she was holding my arm still and let me go. "I mean in Vorentine," she said through clenched teeth, anger snapping in her gray eyes. Her half-elf heritage was showing more than normal, high cheekbones sharp as a blade, her ears, pointed but shorter like her human parent's, peeking out from her thick, dark waves as she turned her head to check the end of the alley where we stood. Like she expected to be interrupted? The act put her beautiful face in sharp relief, shadowed and almost ethereal.

"Working," I said in the same tone, not quite teasing but close enough that she tsked at me when she looked back. Her suspicion about my presence only reinforced the fact that she was, indeed, up to something she felt guilty about.

Please, don't make it my business. As attractive as she was—and as much as Fig thought she might be an interesting choice for me to pursue—my current single status was preferable to attaching myself to any gender.

"Where?" She eased up slightly, though her eyes narrowed as she waited for my response.

"Right there," I said, gesturing at the inn across the street. "How about you?"

She flinched, looking away again. But she didn't get to answer thanks to the sudden appearance of none other than my gnome friend who trotted around the corner into the alley and stopped abruptly with her face lighting up.

"There you are!" It was just like Fig not to read the room and beam a smile at the sullen rogue, looking back and forth between us with a grin that settled into the mischievous. "I should have known you'd track each other down before I could."

Mellie stepped away from me at the same moment I gave her distance, the rogue's startled expression softening her first reaction but not lasting. "Stay out of my way," she snapped at me before spinning on one foot, hands pulling her hood up and over her dark hair, moving off at a pace down the alley toward the other end while I watched her go.

"Did I interrupt something important?" Fig's obvious hurt had me sighing.

"Just the usual rogue drama," I said, looking down at my friend. "Just let her be, all right?"

My little friend shrugged, a flash of irritation showing before she tossed both hands. "If you say so," she said. "But whatever she's up to, that kid she's dealing with is terrible at the sneaking thing, if you ask me."

The fact that even Fig noticed had me frowning and turning toward the end of the now-empty alleyway. "That's Mellie's business," I said absently because my mind now betrayed me with worry for the master rogue. Ridiculous. She could handle herself and had proven as much. Still, something wasn't right and despite my choices to the contrary, sometimes the Yestervere bloodline meant wrangling a sense of right and wrong that really didn't help me maintain my neutrality.

As we emerged from the alley, I realized there was a very good reason that the shadows were longer, the sun going down and now my opportunity to poke my nose in lost regardless. Whatever Mellie and the young man were up to, I had more important things to do, like earning my room and board and hopefully, some tips to go with it.I determinedly retreated to our room to do as I intended, Fig settling into a seat at the bar. When I descended again with my guitar and a few other instruments in tow, I was delighted to see that Soama and Hathin had set up the stage area with the benches I'd noted, three rows of the short seating meaning the tables that encouraged food orders were back from the performance space and only those with drinks would be front and center. Whether they knew it or not, such an arrangement encouraged tipping, though many owners prioritized their own profits over that of the bards who made their living this way.

I liked the pair more and more, honestly, nodding to the smiling innkeepers as they waved at me from behind the bar while I settled on the stool provided and liberated my guitar from its case.

The tavern wasn't full by any means, but the moment I strummed, the wide-open windows meaning the sound could travel to the street, I augmented the notes with a whisper of magic. Music had its own power and with a little boost could reach the most closed of ears and encourage them to pay attention. That meant I was only one verse into my first song when the door opened and a few newcomers entered, quickly joined by others so by the time I had settled myself into the rhythm of how this performance was going to go, it was standing room only at the back.

Now, I always gave my best at every show, don't get me wrong. I chose this life for a reason. Performing, singing, telling stories, and entertaining, all filled me up in ways that nothing else ever had and my very blood and bones sang with me as I poured myself into the songs I shared. But tonight felt even more magical, if only because I truly wished to showcase for the lovely couple who'd welcomed me in a city that didn't feel so kindly.

It wasn't easy being on your own in a place like this. They'd given me a space to share my work in theirs and I was going to ensure that their choice to stand alone was rewarded as much as possible.

That being said, my first set flew by and I was reaching for the mug of watered ale I'd ordered after the last note, swigging it to moisten my dry throat, surprised to find it was time to break. I was usually much better at tracking my time, but tonight I'd submerged myself fully into the music. It wasn't until I blinked back into focus that I realized trouble had returned to Soama and Hathin's taproom, the still-drunk Justes Vorentine perched on the end of the far right bench applauding so hard he spilled his glass of wine all over himself.

"More!" He raised his glass to me. "Encore!"

I was far from done for the night and nodded to him, concern for the innkeepers ending the euphoria of music. "A short break, good sir," I said. "I'll be back."

I stood and was about to head for the bar, though without any plan to help them remove him from their premises, when the door opened and none other than the widow Vorentine walked in.

That could have gone one of two ways. Very, very badly and with guards involved, shutting down the independent inn and tavern under her orders, or.

Or the way it went. Because Soama nodded quickly to me, eyes wide as she rapidly spun to pour a glass of wine for her beleaguered staff, while Theringale observed a moment.

Then strode to the front of the room.

She wasn't alone, as always, though it took her

brother, Justes Uncle Racheff, to vacate the front bench of customers. The black-clad head widow sat front and center, her dark eyes meeting mine, that same flat and empty expression focused on me. I waited for her simpering blonde friend, Yarra Astir, to alight beside her, now dressed in an overly corseted purple and blue gown, Racheff in his dark velvet taking the place on the other side before I nodded slowly to the merchant queen.

And sat back down because it was clear I wasn't getting a break just yet.

Soama left the bar with three drinks on a tray, the taproom falling quiet as the customers all seemed to realize who they had in their midst. So it was a somber moment when the innkeeper bowed a little to the widow and offered her the tray.

"Our finest red, Madam Vorentine," Soama said. "I hope it's to your liking."

The fact that Theringale had even crossed the threshold suggested there was more going on behind the scenes than I was privy to but trust me, I had no plans to disrupt this apparent truce between my hosts and the merchant mistress. When Theringale accepted the drink in a slow and languid motion, that seemed to liberate Yarra to lunge for the second glass, Racheff taking the last one, the only person to acknowledge Soama with a nod of thanks.

Justes watched his mother with a sickly grin, though he made no effort to join her, remaining perched on the bench where he'd begun the night. I did note that he had a lot more room to himself, however, as the two young men who'd been sharing with him melted into the crowd with anxious expressions. Well, I hardly blamed them for their choice to get out of the line of whatever fire that might or might not break out at any second.

With everyone settled, the opening and closing of the main door had me glancing up just long enough to spot the young thief slipping inside, his skulking not improved in the least.

There was a time that I would have chosen to use this opportunity to school Theringale Vorentine for her treatment of the people of her city. Back in the day when I'd first chosen this life, I'd been more impulsive. Let's be fair, I'd been far more like Fig than I cared to admit and wielded my talent like a weapon against those I believed deserved it.

Over the years, however, and thanks to Simon's teaching, I'd discovered that there was a time and a place for songs that bludgeoned and more so for ones that sliced. And, even rarer, times for music that soothed those who I deemed wrongdoers while teaching a lesson that might serve much better. Of course, I'd learned the hard way, more often than not, in the early days, and there were still times when I misjudged those I performed for, though that was much rarer.

I'd come to accept that part of my gift arose from being able to judge what would best serve the moment in time I found myself, and who my music would impact with the greatest benefit. Which was why, instead of playing the song I'd written to humiliate and undercut the woman now seated before me, I made another selection from my repertoire.

"If you'll indulge me," I said, setting aside my guitar for the small lap harp required, "and in honor of our newest guest, allow me to sing you the *Ballad of Amonie the Blue.*"

Theringale's eyes widened just a little, her mouth softening the barest bit. And from the instant I strummed the sweet strings of my harp, I knew I'd won the battle she'd come to wage with a single song.

The power of music, my friend. Why I chose to be a bard.

# CHAPTER TEN

*"Daughter, at last, though many demand,*
*Whatever befalls me, this order will stand.*
*Know that I love you, darling dearest of all*
*With the gift of my fortune, I save you from thrall.*

*Be wealthy and healthy and live all your days*
*As both master and mistress, worthy ever of praise.*
*Good favor and profit be henceforth your lot*
*And to Hel with the others who plunder and plot."*

*She wept for her loss, that faithful daughter and true*
*Child, woman, his heir, Amonie the Blue.*

*Tra-la-loo-ra, tra-la-loo-ra, tra-la-loo-ra-tra-loo*

A bit heavy-handed, perhaps, but the old ballad that told of the death of a famed merchant who, at the time, was pressured to will his business to his younger son, the *Ballad Of Amonie Blue* was a protest against such sexist rules and marked the end of an era in which only males inherited. A hundred years had passed since the death of the now nameless merchant, the bard who'd written it making a heroine of his daughter. And while many songsmiths took liberties with their telling of tales, I knew from being sent to the archives by my mentor to research this very story that not only was Amonie Blue a real woman, she was, indeed, the first of her gender to inherit from her father over her brother. Not only did she take control of his business when he passed, she grew it into one of the most powerful merchant guilds in Valoria, using the proceeds to assist the monarchs of the day in their war to protect themselves from outside aggression. She had a statue to her in the main square of the capital and was awarded a ladyship by the queen of the time for her accomplishments.

You better believe I knew exactly what I was doing when I sang that song to Theringale Vorentine. Did I have any illusions that this widowed woman might have the kind of mettle that made Amonie a heroine in the eyes of Valoria? Honestly, I had no idea. For all I knew, she was the second coming. That wasn't my purpose for performing the old and well-loved ballad.

No, my goal had been utterly transparent and simple—to warm her cold heart, bring a smile to her face even, and maybe, just maybe, soften her toward the lovely young couple who'd welcomed me into their place.

The silence that fell after the performance almost worried me. Theringale had stared the entire time and I didn't break eye contact myself, as though only the two of us existed in that place. When I finally set my strumming hand against the curve of the harp and let the last notes fall still, it felt as though the entire room—the whole world, for that matter—held breath and movement and time itself.

She broke first. Theringale Vorentine hadn't touched her wine, the glass sitting next to her on the bench where she'd deposited it as I'd begun, leaving both of her hands clasped in her lap. She now lifted them slowly to chest height and, slowly and in steady measure, clapped.

It was all the praise I was going to get, but when I nodded to her, she nodded back.

That should have been my victory all wrapped up. I could see her preparing to stand, to leave, as though I'd satisfied something she'd apparently believed required her personal attention. But before she could do so, the door to the tavern burst open.

And the young woman who was Justes' wife stormed in. Shattering the carefully built soft and endearing quiet I'd so meticulously crafted.

Well, it was worth a try, wasn't it?

As for Darmilla, she stomped immediately to her husband's side and started screaming at him.

"What are you doing here?" She grasped for him, jerking him toward her, and he was far too drunk to fight her off. That meant he tipped alarmingly in her direction, about to fall face-first off the bench, only saved by the quick lunge of his uncle. Racheff grabbed Justes by the back of his doublet and pulled him back upright while Darmilla's shrieks continued. "You pathetic, useless—"

"Enough." Theringale stood abruptly, staring down her daughter-in-law who gaped at her in shock.

"You said—" Darmilla didn't back up physically, but I could see her doing so mentally.

"This public humiliation will stop," Theringale said. "Racheff, bring Justes." She didn't even pause as she swept through the gathering. "Darmilla, I expect better."

The head of the Vorentine family paused long enough to deposit something on the bar before exiting in her ground-eating stride as though she wasn't being stared at by everyone in the taproom. It wasn't until she exited that I realized that matron servant of hers had been standing at the entrance the whole time and followed her mistress out. But not before she glanced back over her shoulder and glared at the young thief.

They had a connection that was as obvious as his skulking. I really needed to stop caring what that might be. After all, I'd done my job and now the rest was up to the uncle, it seemed.

A job he didn't relish, Racheff grimacing as he hefted Justes from the bench and half-carried him through the same crowd that gave him all the room he needed. Darmilla stomped one foot before sweeping after them, her cheeks crimson and tears in her eyes while Yarra Astir seemed cruelly amused, winking at me before she followed at a more sedate pace.

When the door finally closed behind them, I felt and heard the collective exhale of relief, though I noted that the young thief didn't waste time going after the Vorentine party as soon as they disappeared.

"Now," I said, breaking the mood and drawing focus on purpose. "I'm going to take that break I earned." The laughter that met my words was followed by a resounding round of applause as the audience released their tension as I intended and the normal chatter of a busy taproom took over.

Despite their clear overwhelm at the bar, Soama hurried to join me, hugging me abruptly then blushing as she let me go. Her flushed face was smiling, dark eyes alight as she wiped her hands on her apron in what felt like an unconscious gesture.

"Thank you," she said, keeping her voice down but clearly excited. "That was incredible." She laughed then, vibrating. "I feared so much what might happen, but you knew exactly what to do. Please, let us pay you tonight for that amazing performance."

"My pleasure," I said with a grin. "We already have an arrangement. I hope my small contribution will make things easier for you going forward."

She squeezed my hand this time, turning back to the bar when Hathin called her name, clearly needing her help. "You've ensured our little place will succeed," she said. "At least, for the time being. And that's so much more than either of us ever expected. Elora Tune, if we can ever do anything for you." She spread her hands in a hopeless gesture, as if unsure as to what that would ever be. "Thank you!" And then she left me to hurry back to her husband and the eager customers who seemed intent on draining their ale casks dry.

I did two more sets before begging off, leaving the happy innkeepers to their now very drunk taproom guests and headed up to bed, yawning as Fig helped me lug my instruments to our room.

It wasn't until she closed the door behind her that she let out a low whistle, bouncing the bag of coins I'd asked her to carry in her little hands.

"Nice haul," she said.

"Good crowd," I agreed, sitting to strip off my boots. The pixie magic had held but my toes weren't happy with the hard pinching required to keep them intact and I wriggled to regain full circulation again.

"Did you see the two bards who came in halfway through your second set?" I had and chose to ignore them and their glaring unhappiness, the way they whispered to one another during my songs, only to be shushed by the surrounding audience.

Such tactics were underhanded means to interrupt and rattle fellow performers. I was more than accustomed to such rudeness from less-than-professional bards and had expected as much. But I'd been doing my job to the satisfaction of the guests because the crowd—the only people that really mattered—had done the work of shutting them down for me.

"So you also saw that big smith in the back toss

one of them into the street?" Fig giggled as I snorted in response.

It helped that the half-orc I'd paid well earlier in the day had my back, of course, Junna's grumpy dwarf partner hefting the second bard over one shoulder and expelling him, too.

That had been the last I'd seen of any interloping songsmiths, which meant word got around. It was almost tempting to stay another night and see what would come of it, if I wasn't eager to get out of Vorentine and back on the road where I belonged.

Pettiness and successful performances were both heady things that combined at times in not the best life choices. Which meant I'd be leaving, of course, as soon as we both had breakfast and leave the vindictive opportunity to prove my worth to others.

Elora Tune had nothing to prove to *anyone*.

A firm knock on the door startled us both, Fig turning so fast the pouch of coins rattled. She quickly tucked it away into the magic strongbox as I rose on stockinged feet and went to find out who wanted what of us so late.

The frowning guard on the other side of the door was familiar, the same one from the gate earlier in the day, in fact. His scowl at Fig was tempered by his task, however, as he nodded to me.

"Madam Vorentine requests your presence, Bard Tune," he said. "For a private performance at Vorentine House."

"How nice," I said. "Tell her I'd be delighted to visit in the morning." I could delay my exit by a few hours if it meant a good payout. I'd made a positive impression and could likely negotiate a solid sum.

Except the guard shook his head, grim as he stepped back and gestured. "Now," he said. "Tonight."

I had the feeling he wasn't going to take no for an answer. And rather than argue—and end up in a fight that I felt Fig tense up to start—I shrugged. Since the last thing I needed was to be kicked out of town thanks to my friend's short temper.

"Can I put on my boots, first?"

## CHAPTER ELEVEN

Fig fidgeted beside me as the large, black carriage rolled through the streets of Vorentine, the interior's plush and comfortable dark velvet seats as delightful as the well-built suspension. The swaying motion along with the clatter of hooves at a steady pace created a rather hypnotic circumstance that lulled me far more than it should have.

Whatever Theringale's intent for this visit, whether to have me entertain—or perhaps something more nefarious—I'd brought only my guitar and the hope that we'd be departing with gold instead of finding ourselves in the subterranean underground of her vast house.

Not that we'd stay there for long, but I hated the thought of having to call in the calvary. Summoning my parents or my bright and boisterous older brother would end up the way I needed but not the way I wanted. As things stood, I was already uncomfortable with the amount of attention I'd stirred up not so long ago in another town and place, far enough from here that I'd avoided being called out for my unique and stellar parentage. Still, all it would take would be a spark to light yet another obvious and obnoxious Yestervere wildfire that certainly would mean, in a place this size, that my anonymity would be severely curtailed in the future.

"What do you think she really wants?" I'd never seen Fig this nervous before, not even on her wedding day. In fact, she'd been a stunning bride and calmer than ever, her husband, Fennel, the anxious one who'd dropped her ring twice as he fumbled his way through his vows. This Fig wasn't the (dare I whisper) arrogant and confident fighter I'd entered Vorentine with, either. Instead, she appeared to be on the verge of panic while she shifted yet again on the velvet seat, feet swinging far too high to reach the floor.

"It's fine," I murmured to her as the carriage slowed. A peek out past the black lace curtains told me we'd arrived at our destination. And we weren't the only ones. As I took in the dark building behind the tall, stone wall with its massive iron gate, the young thief dodged through as the way swung open for our passage.

If he made a mess of my time here, he'd be paying for it.

As for my estimation of the Vorentines—and

whoever had founded this place—they'd done their best to be obvious about their wealth and influence. The stone estate in the center of the city wasn't obvious or anything, was it? It actually amused me maybe more than it should have.

Which, whether warranted or not, had me sitting back and winking at Fig. "I'll sing a few tunes and we'll have a little chat then be on our way."

Fig nodded quickly, though the light from the lanterns caught the white of her eyes as her gaze flickered back and forth. "Sing good, okay?" She let out a little huff of air before laughing breathlessly. "Sorry," she said. "You'll be amazing."

"Thanks for the vote of confidence," I said. "You're okay? You can stay here."

She shook her head, visibly calming. "Rich people make me nervous," she said.

Huh. Since when? She'd spent her young life surrounded by nobility, wealth and power. Where had this anxiety come from?

I alighted from the carriage when the guard opened the door, stepping down like this was my home, not Theringale's, my guitar's strap now draped across my chest and the secured instrument comforting against my back.

"Lead the way," I said, not waiting for the guard to do so.

He hurried to beat me to the obvious entry, the wide stone stairs carrying us up to the massive double doors of what could only be ironwood. Whoever harvested the tree from the Everwilding had also spent a fortune having them carved into an incredible city scape that, I had no doubt, would match perfectly the original version of Vorentine when they were created.

Such shows of fortune and skill didn't impress me past the careful attention of the artisan. Like Fig, I'd been raised at court, after all, my parents beloved of Valoria's monarchs. Not much impressed me, as sad as that might sound, far too jaded to even pause to admire the carvings as I swept through when one of the doors opened before I could pull the cord to alert the staff to our arrival.

Unsurprisingly, the matron who served Theringale greeted me from the other side, nodding to the guard who retreated.

"Bard Tune," the woman said, her soft voice low and measured, "welcome to the Vorentine estate. Madam is waiting for you in the parlor."

That boded well for not being arrested, as far as I was concerned, and I gestured for her to lead the way. "May I have the pleasure of your name, ma'am?"

She seemed surprised that I asked and answered before she could consider her response. "Pim Ulpher," she said.

"A pleasure," I smiled at her. "My companion, Fig Marigold."

Pim flashed a little smile at both of us before her features returned to softly serious. "Madam enjoyed your performance," she said very quietly as she walked us through the towering entry of the estate house, much more castle than mansion, the stone walls etched in patterns and those etchings filled with paint to create a gorgeous landscape inside the vaulted foyer. Remember I said it took a lot to impress me? This did, and now I wondered about the woman who ran this city and if this was something she'd inherited herself or was of her own design. While the towering waterfall over a gushing river and green forest depicted looked lifelike enough I wondered if magic was involved, the paint appeared fresh enough to my eye that it had to have been completely recently.

How long had it been since her husband died? And how long had she waited before she'd begun her remodeling?

Snort.

The parlor's large entrance suggested exactly what I expected, though the lovely glass space on the other side was even larger than the one the king and queen kept private audience in. I immediately noted that though the rest of her people seemed to be in attendance, the lady of the hour wasn't.

Yarra Astir wiggled her fingers at me over the rim of her cup, already changed yet again into a full robe of red velvet and pure white fur, her blonde ringlets set in a rather elaborate updo for what amounted to fancy pajamas.

"The bard," she breathed in snarky excitement, "has arrived."

Justes stirred, clearly coming down from his inebriation, though he straightened, pulling himself together far more quickly than should have been possible. Unless, of course, this state of drunkenness was his usual, in which case no doubt his body had adapted to it.

Darmilla shot him a furious look before nodding to me. "I didn't get to hear you play," she said, the faint complaint in her tone aimed, not at me, but at the rest of the gathering. All of whom ignored her.

"Bard Tune," Racheff approached me, holding out one hand, his grasp firm and commanding, though he seemed as steady and collected as I'd first guessed. I glanced down at his wrist, noting the scars there, and knew my suspicions about his origins were correct. Those faint marks came from the repeated impact of a sword's guard and meant he chose to swing a rapier without the benefit of a glove for protection.

My brother Thune would adore him.

"Good sir," I said.

"Racheff Sargot," he told me, completing his identity at last. "Please, come in. My sister will be with us presently. Forgive the lateness of the hour, but she keeps long days and rarely gets to enjoy herself." He guided me to a stool that had been set beside the massive stone hearth, voice dropping as he went on. "She truly appreciated your talent and very much appreciates your willingness to entertain her on her terms."

While I doubted she'd have said as much, I took his assurance at face value and smiled. "My pleasure," I said, unslinging my guitar and freeing the instrument before Fig took the case away. I was surprised that she simply stood off to one side with the tall black leather in front of her, almost like a shield. Nor did my normally chatty friend attempt to say a word.

I played a few songs, nothing too heavy, when Racheff encouraged me to do so.

"My sister will be along shortly," he said, frowning when Darmilla exited in a rush. She returned a few moments later as I finished my first tune, only for Yarra to rise and go as well, followed by a staggering Justes. I expected his wife to attend him, but she turned her face away and stared out the glass into the darkness on the other side, face pinched and angry. Only when Yarra returned did Racheff frown and bow a little to me.

"I'll check on Theringale," he said, departing. Justes returned a moment later, leaning on the matron, Pim Ulpher, who left him sagging in a chair with his head resting on one propped up fist.

I almost lost the lyrics when I spotted someone creeping past the glass wall just out of sight and had to jerk myself back from a spontaneous reaction. The young thief hadn't yet been spotted, it turned out, and now I questioned the quality of Theringale's guards if he'd been able to wander about in such ridiculous fashion without being caught or challenged.

When a half-turning had passed and there was still no sign of the lady of the house, I had to smother a yawn as I tried to decide on the next song to sing. Only to look up as Racheff entered, frowning and shaking his head at me.

"My apologies," he said. "My sister is… unavailable." His hesitation had me stiffening a little, but he spread his hands and smiled grimly. "Perhaps another time."

Yarra snickered and finished her drink with a single toss, setting her glass aside. "Theringale is far too busy for a silly bard anyway," she said before flouncing her way out of the room.

Racheff frowned at the comment but didn't correct the horrible woman, instead offering me a pouch which Fig rushed forward to claim. He seemed surprised she was even there, like he'd forgotten her entirely but handed it over regardless.

"For your troubles," he said. "The carriage will take you back again, Bard Tune. Thank you for your time and safe travels." He exited again before I could ask a question, Justes standing and belching loudly before wandering off. Only Darmilla remained, though she was still a stiff statue staring out into the night, the opposite direction the young thief had gone, though as I packed up my guitar in silence, I noted the tears running down her cheeks and her small, furtive motions to wipe them away and realized she wouldn't have seen him even if he had chosen that side to creep.

Poor thing.

"Let's go," I said, leading the way, my guitar in my hand instead of over my back, ready to just get out of this place. As beautiful as the interior was, as much as I now wondered who Theringale could be behind her cold façade, I found I no longer cared.

She and her family of misery were about to be behind me, and it would be many a season before I darkened the gates of Vorentine again. If it was even called that by the time I returned.

Fig had brightened somewhat, glancing back as

Pim Ulpher opened the door for us, allowing us to exit.

"Is it just me," she said in a quiet voice that none the less sounded a lot more like her than it had all day, "or is that place the creepiest you've ever been in?"

I'd been in some very creepy places but I just grinned.

"Sleep," I said, "breakfast." *Boots*, my feet reminded me. "And the road."

She nodded happily, reaching up to jerk open the door of the carriage, a long reach for her. I almost missed that they had swapped out the more elaborate and massive black one for the blue-toned rig for the ride back, but I wasn't about to make a fuss. "Good riddance," she muttered.

Her relief turned to a faint mouse-squeak as, when the door popped open, something pale fell out.

A hand. Wearing a ring bearing a crest I recognized, of course. And just past it, staring, empty eyes that seemed far more surprised than they ever had in life.

"Theringale," Fig breathed in horror.

I guess now we knew what kept her.

# CHAPTER TWELVE

Just what I needed, another murder to contend with. What were the odds we could just hit the road and get out of town before anyone found out the city's matriarch was dead?

Slim to none, apparently, someone letting out a thin scream behind us. I turned to find that Pim had emerged from the house and was pointing at the obvious as she then spun and raced back inside. While a pair of guards hustled forward from the doorway toward us.

"Don't move!" That was the guard from the gate who took one look at the dead woman in the carriage and leveled his pike at me. "You're under arrest."

And this night just took a turn for the oh *heck* no. Because like it or not, I wasn't going down for something I didn't do in a city that could arrest me and toss me into a hole so deep it would take the entire legion of the Paladins of Light and Liberty to dig me out again.

Without a trial, no less.

I immediately waved the man off, glaring, and knowing what it meant, reached into my leather jacket. With a whisper of music and magic, I summoned the Guild badge from the secret box it normally rode in, irritated when it took form in my palm as much as I was grateful for its presence. It wriggled like an eager puppy that had been waiting for just this opportunity, and probably altered my parents the instant I called for it. Well, there wasn't much I could do about that at the moment. I pulled the shining, shimmering thing free of its supposed hiding place and flashed it to the approaching guards.

Who froze in place when it glittered and glistened in response to my touch.

Sigh. Show off.

"Guild Bard Master Elora Tune," I said. "Don't even think about it."

Things couldn't possibly get worse. This was the last line I wanted to cross. And as the Vorentine collective came running out of the house and down the steps, each of them taking a turn staring at the dead woman in the carriage and then my badge, it was clear that no one here had the faintest idea what to do with me.

"Why is a Guild Master in a freehold city?" Leave it to Racheff Sargot to bring up that detail. Not that

Guild wasn't allowed in Vorentine, but it wasn't an official welcome by any means and though I had standing, it had to be authenticated and accepted by those in power in a merchant freehold to help at all.

And hopefully not hinder.

"I'm performing," I said through clenched teeth. "I'm a bard."

His previous attitude seemed to have shifted somewhat. "Spying, more likely," he said. "Did my sister discover your deceit and you killed her for it?"

Now he was being ridiculous, Yarra gasping (though her shock had obviously turned to fake grief barely hiding her eager interest) and Darmilla shaking where she stood a few feet away, hands over her mouth. Only Justes seemed unable to accept what he was dealing with, Pim Ulpher's initial reaction of angst suppressed as she rushed forward to support him. The young man swayed and shook his head.

"Is that Mother?" He blinked at me. "Is my mother dead?"

Maybe flashing my badge hadn't been the greatest decision, because now Racheff was stepping back, reaching out to unsheath a sword from the side of one of the guards. He might have been a rapier man but he certainly knew how to handle a short sword and pointed the business end in my direction as he scowled.

"Come quietly," he said. "Answer our questions or this will end badly for you."

"How *dare* you," Fig snapped at him, her confidence returning at the very worst possible time.

"Do you have any idea who she is?" I didn't get to shut her up. I wished I had, but it was far too late and I'd been distracted with my own bad decision, so turning toward her as she finished her angry retort out loud was all I could manage. "This is Elora Tune *Yestervere*," she snarled, "and you're *way* out of line. Now put that sword away and stop being an idiot."

I choked but hoped I didn't show it as the Vorentine contingent all stared at me in shock. I thought they'd been surprised when I flashed my badge. This might have been a freehold, but even they knew the surname my parents gave me at birth, not to mention the fabled and legendary epic awesomeness that went along with it.

Ahem. Sarcasm had no place in the moment, but I couldn't help it.

Racheff backed down immediately, even if Yarra hesitated a moment before prodding him.

"So she says," she hissed. "You believe her?"

He hesitated while I exhaled a long breath and contemplated throttling my little gnome friend for exposing me like this, her smug expression paired with firmly crossed arms.

I didn't have a choice. Teeth gritted, I pushed power into the badge and let its internal magic trigger confirmation of my identity. You can bet it trilled a happy song when I did. The happy wriggle it made in my palm when I'd called it was nothing compared to its bliss out at being asked to prove who I was.

Magic was ridiculous sometimes, especially when embedded in objects that had no business being sentient.

And yet, it saved my bacon, didn't it? While it might have been possible to break the seal on Guild badges to steal someone's credentials, I'd never encountered the means and Racheff seemed to feel the same, the sword returned to the guard while the victim's brother nodded to me.

Still scowling.

"I'll ask again," he said, though with less aggression, "what's a Yestervere—"

"Playing," I snapped, tucking my badge away as it continued to hum its happiness against my chest, wincing over the fact that my parents would be calling on me any second now, especially since I'd been forced to prove my identity the way I had. Suddenly, I wished I'd allowed him to arrest me. "Your sister invited me." Did I really have to remind him of that?

He didn't get to respond because power flooded me and I knew from the flare of light that glowed on everyone's faces—and the front of the house, the grass, the general vicinity—that Mom and Dad had landed.

Just as they flared out of the giant glowing patch of magic they'd sent and blazed into life beside me. Oh, they'd read the room all right. They'd made the assumption that my need for proof of my identity demanded the kind of entrance that no one could deny. Except, of course, it only made things so much worse.

I loved them, I really did. But fanfare? A light show? Just… sigh.

"Guild Master Bard," Mom said.

"Dearest daughter and light of our lives," Dad said.

I didn't gag. Or laugh. In fact, this was all so completely unhinged that I just stood there and tried not to eye roll.

It worked though, didn't it? Of course, it did. The Vorentines backed off while I flexed my jaw from the ache of gritting my teeth and turned to the projections of my parents.

"*Was* that necessary?" I didn't ask very loudly, just enough to reach them.

"We assumed you required confirmation," Mom answered just as quietly. I'd just been through this in my own mind, but her contrition was admirable.

"You tapped into your real identity," Dad said, glancing at my mother.

"It's fine," I said. It wasn't, but whatever. This wasn't their fault and they didn't deserve to be treated badly because I had to take certain steps that made me uncomfortable. "I've found myself in a rather awkward position."

"Again," Fig piped up. "Hello, Amara, Endile."

They smiled at her while I waited. Breathed. I didn't look at Fig. Took a lot, but whatever. Why did that make them look so happy? They could have at least tried to hide their enthusiasm.

"Show me," Mom said. I spun and gestured at the body in the carriage while she nodded without regret or empathy. "Understood," she said. "Guild Master Bard Elora Yestervere, the Guild charges you with uncovering the truth behind the death of… who is she, sweetie?"

"Theringale Vorentine," I said.

"Elora," Dad said with a growing frown on his handsome face. "Why are you in a freehold city?"

"Not now, Endile," Mom said softly, barely moving her lips before going on in that vibrant voice of hers. "Very well. With the permission of the heir to the freehold?"

I turned and gestured at Justes. He seemed shocked to be pointed out, even appeared unhappily sober as Darmilla pushed him toward me.

"Um, sorry, what?" He blinked at my parents and then back at me. "You're just a bard," he said in a whining voice.

"I assure you, sir," Dad said at his most commanding, the warrior wizard high elf general (so many titles, Dad) coming out in his tone and demeanor, "Guild Master Yestervere is more than capable of the task." He grimaced a little. "With your leave, she will assist your guard in the investigation of Theringale Vorentine's…" Dad glanced at me. "Untimely death?"

Likely a murder, but I didn't know for sure. I just nodded, knowing I had to look grim but not because of the subject matter, per se. More out of intense frustration and fury.

Justes wavered on his feet. "Do what you want," he said. "I can't stop you."

Actually, he could, but it was probably better he didn't know that. And no one seemed willing to inform him, so… I guess I was on the case, then.

His uncle did seem concerned about one thing, however. "Son," Racheff said gently and sadly, "with your mother deceased, you're now the heir to the Vorentine merchant empire."

The young man seemed shocked by that, even laughing a little before his uncle's steady, dark stare made him stop. Justes swallowed hard before his eyes met mine, panic there making me wonder if it was an act to keep him from the suspect list or the truth.

"Of course," he said after spluttering a few words that didn't sound coherent enough to translate. And only came out with those two when Darmilla poked him hard from where she'd come up behind her husband to do so. "Proceed." He gestured, the movement ridiculous and I think even he knew it. Justes retreated while his wife met my eyes with her pale ones full of anxiety before she turned and followed him.

I stepped aside then as the rest of them backed away, even Racheff, though he watched me carefully as I turned and conversed with my parents.

"Fig," Mom said with a smile, and only then did I realize my friend was beside me. "I hear congratulations are in order on your first campaign. Well done."

My parents had always treated my best friend like a treasured part of our family. And yet, it was kind of them to have followed her exploits considering how busy they both were. I wasn't sure I'd have been as thoughtful in their position.

"Thanks, Amara," Fig said as brightly as ever, dimples showing. "Elora's way more fun, though."

The three of them laughed. Yes, I was sour about it.

"Keeping our girl out of trouble, I see," Dad chuckled.

"If you don't mind," I said.

Dad cleared his throat, still obviously amused. Mom disappeared for a moment from the magic while he seemed to be listening to something before he nodded and refocused on me. "You're in charge of the investigation officially," he said, "so keep us posted, Elora."

Mom reappeared, looking pleased. "We're going to send you some backup regardless," she said. "Freeholds can be tricky politically and we want to be sure you aren't on your own out there, sweetie." She shrugged. "We trust you, of course, but you should have someone accustomed to the possible issues that could arise in such an investigation."

My mother might have been a powerful sea elf sorcerer who'd saved her home island from the Kraken before she met dad, but she loved her politics.

"Not Thune then," I said, the thought of my older brother landing here with his shining Light and unicorn partner, Cloudest, only increasing the odds that something not exactly ideal might come of the proceedings.

Dad laughed as Mom shook her head.

"While your brother's Order requires his presence," she said (in other words, not a freaking chance), "it turns out your sister is available."

I almost choked. "Posh?" The oldest of us and the most decorated master rogue to ever join the Guild, designated Queen's Rogue after she rescued the heir to the throne single-handedly?

That—gulp—amazing and intimidating sister?

"Exactly," Mom said. "I told her where you are. She'll portal in shortly."

Oh, *goody*.

Fine, the truth.

Oh, *no*.

## CHAPTER THIRTEEN

Do not get me wrong. I loved my sister. Posh was the kind of elder sibling that literal songs were written about. So was my brother, Thune, of course, but the epic rogue who was twenty years my elder had already been kicking rear ends and taking names by the time I came around, diving into her first adventure at the tender age of fifteen. And not with an experienced group, either, but one she'd put together of her closest friends from her grade group, the five of the mid-teens sneaking into the Everwilding and liberating a previously stolen icon taken from the Temple of Lya Herself by none other than the Kobold Consortium. That most notorious and nasty collection of thieves in the entire world, their leader not just the best thief in the business but known for decimating his enemies and putting them on display for their temerity in challenging him.

You read that right. *Fifteen.* She took him on like he was a mere inconvenience. And returned the Goddess icon personally to the temple. Oh, but there's more. Posh did so without fanfare. Under full anonymity, swearing her companions to secrecy, she and her friends accomplished what no one else could. The only way anyone found out it had been Posh was five years later because one of her company had let it slip during a drunken card game he was losing.

And when the High Priestess of Lya tried to celebrate my sister for her accomplishment? Posh refused the accolade and instead donated the reward money to a widow and orphan fund that helped borderland families who lost their loved ones to that same consortium's attacks.

*That* was Posh Yestervere. And no, I wasn't saying that my sister was a saint or perfect or anything like that (despite wondering myself if it might be true). She had her faults (I think) and her foibles (maybe, though debatable) and while her profession implied an inherent nature of chaos and compatibility with skirting the law, Posh's reputation spoke much louder than words. Her acts over her career (that was far from over) reinforced that first victory rather than contradicting it. Up to and including her rescue of the heir to the throne that earned her the title she now carried of Queen's Rogue. A title that hadn't existed before and would likely die with her.

Yes, that was my big sis. When she went back and

took out the Kobold leader ten years later, no one was surprised that he fell to her and that her act crumbled the consortium into dust when she dragged him to justice all by her lonesome.

I loved my sister. Everyone did with very good reason. She wasn't arrogant or condescending or obtuse. Posh was exactly as she presented herself and never once to my knowledge accepted any less than the best from herself.

The truth was, I wasn't worried about her joining me because she'd belittle me or make my life difficult. If anything, she was the perfect choice for the matter. No, if anything, the reason I dreaded her arrival had nothing to do with Posh and everything to do with personal judgment.

I was just terrified of disappointing her.

Do you really blame me?

That meant there was only one thing to do. I had to get to work and sort as much out as I could before she arrived so I didn't embarrass myself. Fig's delight wasn't helping matters, though, my little friend practically bouncing in her boots as her wide eyes met mine.

I turned back to my parents and nodded, hoping they didn't see the anxiety on my face. "I'll be waiting," I said, cutting them off before either of them could speak again. They let me, too, not trying to maintain the connection though they certainly could have done so. I was grateful they didn't push the point or the moment, letting me do what I needed to do as they said they would.

This case was mine. A case I didn't want, mind you, but now had no choice but to accept. At least, until my amazing sister arrived. Because there was always that option, wasn't there? Hand the reins over to Posh and walk?

Trust me, I considered it. Insidious whispers in my head that she'd judge me for such a choice had me spinning to face the Vorentine collective again, shoulders back and jaw aching from the perpetual clench.

"Everyone," I said, "inside." I looked down again at Fig, lowering my voice. "We need to locate the young man who's been following Theringale."

"Mellie's friend?" She nodded immediately. "I'll track her down."

It turned out there was no need to do so. As Racheff and the guards guided the family back into the house on my command, I realized that the rogue in question had already arrived, Mellie lurking near the carriage containing the body. It was clear that she'd already had a look at the widow's corpse and was waiting for me to notice her. How she'd known there was trouble had only one answer and I was scowling as I crossed to her.

"You knew," I said.

Mellie's sullen expression wasn't helping matters. "Ferrick had nothing to do with this," she said. Before hesitating because now I had the young thief's name.

"He's been following the victim," I said, an unnecessary reminder that made her tsk softly. When she shifted out into the light, I noted that she wore her own badge front and center, as though she'd anticipated needing it.

"Let me talk to him," she said. Was that desperation in her voice?

"Just as soon as I have him in custody," I said. "Me first. Then again, unless you're willing to assist in making that happen, you can forget it."

Whatever connection she had, whether as his mentor or not, Mellie's distress was real, I couldn't argue that.

"I'll bring him to you," she said. "But only if you'll listen to what he has to say. And not jump to conclusions."

"You're pushing the boundaries of any kind of demands you've earned," I said. "Master Rogue or not, the fact that you're involved with a suspect negates your rights to be involved, Mellie."

"I know that," she said, voice lowering as her gaze did, too. I'd seen her relent like this the last time we'd worked together, when she discovered who I was, though she'd quickly recovered her attitude. About faces were her specialty if it meant she got what she wanted. All right, maybe that was mean and uncalled for, but I wasn't in the mood to deal with her manipulation tactics. "His name is Ferrick Ulpher," she said, giving me a second to make the connection that didn't need longer than a breath. I'd already seen him interact with the matron servant of the victim, hadn't I? So the reveal that they were related—likely mother and son—wasn't all that surprising. "And he's tied to this family in ways that haven't been acknowledged."

That I hadn't anticipated and made me leap to a conclusion she implied. "A familial connection?"

Mellie backed off. "I'll bring him to you," she said. "You'll hear him out." Not a question this time.

I let her go without acknowledging either way, watching her pause and nervously recognize that I wasn't promising anything before she disappeared into the darkness.

While Fig sighed deeply. "I changed my mind," she said. "That girl is nothing but trouble."

She could say that again.

I took a moment to step up and give the victim a look, confirming to myself that the cause of death warranted calling it murder. Unless, that was, the slim-bladed poignard protruding from under her right arm was a self-inflicted wound. Right, because stabbing oneself in the armpit in exactly the place where it would penetrate the heart was something Theringale would have done to herself.

The black fabric of her dress hid any gore, but it was obvious to me that the killer had known what they were doing to stab her so efficiently. I couldn't see any distinguishing marks on the hilt, the plain and serviceable weapon wiped clean magically when I whistled a short tune over it.

Exactly what a trained rogue would do to hide their tracks after an assassination.

"Let's go inside and talk to the family," I said as I stepped down. While the young man hadn't shown much aptitude in sneaking, who knew if his talents lay elsewhere? Like, in stabbing widows and leaving them in carriages? "If Mellie doesn't deliver the young man in question by the time we're done, we'll go looking for him ourselves." Or I could send Posh after him.

The very idea of sending my sister under my orders to do anything had me wincing as I backed up and, magic in my voice, sang a soft song at the carriage. My music sealed the victim inside until I could bring in a healer to more fully examine her, preserving the evidence behind my power and ensuring if anyone tried to interfere with it, I'd know it instantly.

As would they since I embedded a lovely little banshee seal in the shield that would burst the eardrums of any sneak who didn't know better.

The remains protected and a young guard sent for the local cleric, I turned and entered the house again, Fig on my heels lugging my guitar with her and freeing me from that task, doing my best to portray outward confidence that I really hoped convinced the rest of the world I knew what I was doing.

I just wished the looming arrival of my sister didn't make me feel the opposite.

# CHAPTER FOURTEEN

Racheff greeted me as I entered the foyer, clearly not understanding that he was as much a suspect as anyone in the death of his sister. Then again, his grim expression as he stepped aside and let me command the guards who seemed confused and concerned when he did so suggested otherwise.

"I'll be in the library," he said to me. "Awaiting your questions." He spun and strode off, the guard from the gate following him and standing outside the doorway he passed through as though already given orders to do just that.

How efficient. And had me dropping Racheff lower on the list of suspects, even as my anxious mind whispered to me that wouldn't a murderer do so to allay suspicions?

"Go with him," I said to my little gnome friend. She nodded immediately and did as I asked. Was I being overly cautious? Maybe. Second-guessing myself was going to be a problem. Or not.

Oh, boy.

Instead of letting my traitor brain get the better of me, I marched to the first door under guard, the entry to the parlor where I'd been earlier performing and nodded to the young woman there on my way through.

It turned out this was the room where Yarra Astir had been segregated. The moment I appeared, she transformed from lounging in a chair with a drink in her hand, the flicker of her boredom briefly visible, to weeping openly and wailing a little.

"You have to find out who did this to my dear Theringale!" She collapsed backward into the plush seat, her performance ridiculously extravagant considering the attitude I'd caught her in. "What a tragic end to a truly amazing woman."

I didn't respond, letting her absorb my displeased expression. The thing about giving suspects time to realize they weren't fooling anyone was that often the less practiced and more gullible were likely to crack and say something they didn't intend to. Not so in Yarra's case. She continued to blubber and stare at me, our battle of momentary wills at a standstill.

Very well, a new tactic then. "I'm very sorry for your loss," I conceded. "Tell me, Madam Astir, who do you believe would ever want to bring harm to Theringale Vorentine?"

I'd chosen well, of course, and whether she knew I'd read her easily or not, Yarra's eagerness to spill all the dirt she had seemed far stronger than any sense of self-preservation.

Her grief slipped enough that she was able to lean forward, that drink still in her hand, a coyish tilt to her head though she did maintain her sad moue of concern. "This whole family," she gushed, one hand pressing to her abundant chest. "My poor, dear Theringale had her hands full."

"Do tell," I said and let her go on.

Which she did abundantly. "Don't get me started on that son of hers," she said. "If Justes' father was still alive, he'd be devastated at the state of the boy." She huffed a little, sipping her drink, eyes bright with delight at finally being able to talk, no doubt. "He's already emptied half the wine cellar and galivants about in the city doing the same to the more expensive taprooms. The reason he was slumming it in an independent establishment yesterday. No one beholden to Theringale would serve him any longer."

How interesting. "He's her only heir?"

Yarra's eyes widened as she nodded like this was some probative information instead of the obvious. "He and that guttersnipe of a wife of his," she said, voice lowering, not exactly secretive but definitely weighted for cruelty and conniving. "Darmilla's ambitions were the only reason Justes fell for her, the poor lamb." Yarra's flip-flopping between blame and sympathy said so much about her that I was now doubtful anything she told me could be taken at face value. Still, if her gossip led me down roads I could investigate from more reliable sources, so be it. "The nasty tart hates all of us, I'm sure of it. Including the husband she saddled herself with." Yarra inhaled a long breath, letting out a gust of sound that was all judgment. "As for Racheff, her brother is a weak yes man in his sister's employ, broken and useless otherwise since he returned from adventuring a few years ago." She paused to sip again. "I hear he was the reason his last campaign failed and all of his companions died in the Everwilding."

That kind of tragic end to a career could tend to warp a soul, but I hadn't gotten that impression from Racheff, so I was holding off my own opinions until I spoke to him directly. I would be, however, inquiring with the Guild if his company had been registered and what outcome had befallen his last campaign.

"What happened to Theringale's husband?" His recent death could be tied to this, or it might have just been a coincidence. It served me to ask, however. Yarra's lack of surprise was as honest an expression as she'd ever shown. So, she also thought the deaths might be connected. Interesting.

"Balmont," the woman said with what was no doubt meant to be a sage nod to me. "Another horrible loss amid mysterious circumstances." She wiggled her fingers in some implication of magic, perhaps, or at the very least mischief. "The fact he liked to step out on Theringale always made me wonder what really happened."

That aside that was as much an accusation as

anything else she'd said only confirmed the leap of conclusion I'd made earlier with Mellie, but I wanted the truth from the actual subjects in question so I let her go on.

"In fact," Yarra said, "there's always been a rumor that there's a second heir. Another son of Balmont's who, should he come and claim his birthright, would have been rewarded for it."

"Liar!" I should have been more careful, I suppose, but I'd left the guard at the door to do her duty. So the sudden appearance and screaming accusation from Justes as he burst into the room had me kicking myself for not being more cautious.

He lunged for the woman in the chair, Yarra's honest reaction one of fear as she scrambled out of his way, though I could tell from the faintest smile that arose she was secretly delighting in winding him up. Since he staggered in his attempt to attack her, stumbling over the corner of the rug and face-planting into the back of another chair, her amusement barely disguised by fake concern was clearly the accurate of the two expressions.

And had her right at the top of my suspect list whether she knew it or not.

"Liar," he repeated, voice muffled in the fabric of the seat he tried to push himself up and away from only to have his knees give way, his body weight carrying him to the floor where he collapsed, weeping. "You're *lying*!"

"Justes!" Darmilla rushed in next while I spun and glared at the two guards standing just inside the door.

They both ducked out again, clearly unwilling to stand up against their new employer and his wife and, to be fair, I guess I understood their reaction. After all, I was only here until I found out who killed Theringale. They'd have to answer for their actions to Justes and Darmilla for a long time to come.

That was unless one or both of them were hanged for killing Theringale. The guards weren't taking any chances they were innocent.

That put me at a distinct disadvantage, however, leaving me to handle things. Until Posh arrived, that was, I reminded myself. My luck, right in the middle of me fumbling a murder investigation.

Darmilla, meanwhile, crouched next to her husband, glaring at Yarra who hovered near the fireplace. "You nasty witch!" When Justes reached for his wife, however, she stood and backed up, the drunken heir tumbling over onto the floor again. "How dare you open your mouth and gossip about this family. Master Bard, you can't trust a word that comes out of this wretched woman's mouth."

I'd already come to that conclusion but didn't say so out loud. "Madam Vorentine," I said, "I'll be with you and your husband shortly."

"I couldn't just let her malign us," Darmilla said, tears standing in her eyes. She gestured vaguely at her husband. "I know how this looks, but he's a good person. Neither of us would ever—"

"Oh, *please*," Yarra said, condescending tone as biting as the poignard that killed Theringale, "*spare* us, Darmilla. Everyone knows you married Justes for his money."

"At least I was honest," the young woman snapped back. "I don't pretend to be friends with Theringale only to take advantage of her at every turn." She stepped away further when Justes groaned and again tried to leverage himself off the floor, his hands catching at the hem of her red gown. Darmilla's open horror shone in her eyes, written on her young face. "If this family is falling apart," she said, "I blame you, you terrible old windbag."

Yarra snarled at her, shifting into attack mode, her attempts to hide her true nature snapping in half as she lunged for the younger woman. Fig was faster than me, getting between them, but it was obvious to me that neither of them were going to be easy to talk to while in the same room together.

"I'll handle this," Fig said. Wait, what was she doing there? She was supposed to be watching over Racheff. Who, it turned out, had joined the watching crowd, no surprise, I suppose. I didn't debate with my gnome friend about her inability to do as I asked, allowing her to corner Yarra while I motioned for the peeking guards to come inside and help their master to his feet. Which they did, while Darmilla watched, that same aghast expression almost like regret but much more so to me like the face of a woman who couldn't believe what she'd sacrificed to end up like this.

"Madam Vorentine," I said. "If you please."

She shuddered and nodded, heading for the door at a clip, passing her husband. Justes couldn't walk on his own, supported by two guards, disappearing into the foyer as I followed. I didn't miss the lurking and nervous matron, Pim Ulpher, who no one had thought to segregate.

And now I really *was* frustrated because I'd been fumbling this whole thing from the get-go. Well, I hadn't been planning on running a murder investigation with just Fig for backup, had I?

Good thing then, I guess, that a burst of magic sent me toward the front door, where a portal surged into view, rainbow light tinted faintly red. Shimmering as the tall, slim and stunning vision of rogue epicness who was my sister strode through.

It *was* a good thing, right?

## CHAPTER FIFTEEN

I only peripherally realized that Posh wasn't alone, only because she spotted me as though fully expecting me to be right where she found me, a smile on her face and her arms opening for a hug.

Her embrace was as warm and engulfing as ever, the smooth black leather of her uniform soft and pliable, the cloak she wore as light as a feather as though made of shadow. When my brother, Thune, hugged me, it was like Light itself wrapped around me and smothered me in its heat while his arms crushed me against the metal plate he wore so proudly. Posh's quiet darkness was no less suffocating but had a delicate deliberateness to it that felt intrusive without being overt, as though she learned every single one of my secrets with a simple touch.

And yet, Posh gave the best hugs so who was I to argue with the dichotomy of the experience?

She released me with that smile still lingering, though it was grimmer than before, her dark blue eyes more a match to our sea elf mother's, matching deep blue hair sleek like hers in a thick braid coiled at the nape of her neck. Her pale, flawless skin looked sculpted, arching brows following the sharp line to the impressive points of her ears in perfect symmetry. The fact that I'd leaned into the red in my locks, the green of my mother's gaze and taken on as much of a differing appearance from my siblings as possible was never so obvious as when I stood in my sister's presence.

Posh wasn't just the best at what she did, she was the ideal distillation of both of our gorgeous parents and carried her beauty and poise with a natural confidence that demanded respect without asking for it.

Argh. Did I mention I loved my sister but she made me very, very nervous?

"Elora," she said in her deep alto. "Well met, sister."

"Hello, Posh," I said. "Nice to see you."

"And you." She looked up, the six inches she and Thune had on me always making me feel like the runt of the litter (that I was, let's be fair), gaze taking in the entry of the manor before she turned and noted the carriage behind her. "The crime scene?"

I nodded. "I've sealed it, waiting on a cleric."

The two rogues who'd come with her grinned and

waved at me, their attitudes much different from my sister's, though she seemed indulgent with them as she gestured them forward.

"Elora, my finest team joined me to assist you." The feralfolk twins surprised me, far more frequent near the border than enrolling in rogue training. "Lans," the hare adapted of the pair bobbed his head, long ears flopping though there was nothing comical about his confident stance or how his careful gaze continually flickered around us, "and Lire Briarbridge." His fox-like sister saluted me, amber gaze as mischievous as her smile, though, like her brother, she seemed to have earned Posh's respect for good reason, her lack of tension and loose, fluid movements as steadily assured as her brother's. As with all feralfolk, the set of twins was of mismatched influence but I had little doubt that their inherited gifts complemented one another perfectly.

"Master Bard," Lans and Lire said in unison.

"Nice to meet you," I said. And suddenly, despite my reservations and near-panic attack over the thought, I was glad Posh had come and brought her team with her.

"Thune tells me you're making this a habit," my sister said with amusement in her voice, though she waved off my protest before I could voice it. "Circumstances as they are, what do you need from us, Master Bard Tune?"

She didn't call me Yestervere. That Posh, acknowledging and embracing my boundaries without making a big show of it. Why was I worried again? Oh, and hang on.

"I thought you might like to take over," I said.

Posh snorted, the feralfolk siblings exchanging a look. "I understand you've been assigned this case," my sister said. "We're here as your team. So, again, once you know where you want us and what you need, consider it done."

And just like that, she put more weight on my shoulders while doing her best not to. Because by reinforcing what Mom and Dad said, she assured me she had no interest in undercutting my authority. Authority I didn't want, remember? Even as she basically told me she was ready when I was ready, no pressure or anything. Was it just me or did that just feel like I needed to hurry up and do something already?

Cue panic attack again, gotcha. Something Posh would never, ever see.

"If you two could watch the carriage until the cleric arrives," I said to Lans and Lire in a firm voice that only shook in my head, "you and I," I turned my attention back to my sister, "can talk to rest of the family while I wait on another Guild agent," I almost stumbled over that, thinking of Mellie, wondering if Posh knew her, realizing she likely did and not sure why that made me even more nervous, even as I hoped Mellie wouldn't let me down and run off with Ferrick Ulpher, "to bring in the last of the suspects."

Can you tell my mind was racing? Let me make it clearer if you missed it. Racing like a long-boned wirewolf who hadn't eaten for a fortnight. Did I smell like anxiety? Surely, the pair of feralfolk could scent such things. If so, they didn't make me aware of it.

"Of course." Lans and Lire bobbed nods instead, spinning together and circling the carriage. I removed my magic with a soft whistle, knowing it would take a moved mountain for anyone to get past those two and needing the victim accessible to the healer when they arrived. This way I wouldn't have to come running at an inopportune time and freed me from that possible embarrassment.

Why I was so worried about such things stood waiting for me to lead her into the house and I managed a smile for her despite my internal tumbling routine that involved a handful of fluttersprites drunk on elderberry nectar.

"Lead the way," Posh said.

I had nothing and everything to prove as I did just that.

## CHAPTER SIXTEEN

Fig squealed at the sight of Posh who laughed and crouched to hug my friend without reservation despite the watching guards who muttered among themselves. It was obvious to me that they knew exactly who my sister was, and that while they might not have been willing to do as I said in the face of the family's displeasure, they'd think twice about going against the Queen's Rogue the same way.

Didn't hit my ego where it hurt or anything.

Fig grinned as she let Posh go, elbowing me. "Look at us," she said, "on an adventure together." I knew that had always been one of my gnome friend's wildest dreams, though to make it truly complete my parents and Thune would be here, but it had to have been clouding her judgment (I mean, tickling her pink) considering how new she was to her chosen redirect in career.

My sister nodded. "About time," she said as though this were the epitome for her, too, because that was Posh, being all-inclusive and meaning everything she said with an honesty and quiet stoicness that made everyone feel like her peer. Hang on a second, why was she looking at me like that?

I didn't wait to find out what her steady stare intended, clearing my throat and quickly and quietly filled her in on everything I knew. Posh didn't ask questions, simply waiting for me to empty out my reservoir of information. She seemed to think over the information before nodding.

"Thorough," she said. "Now what?" Why did she have to make that sound like an instructor asking a student without even intending to? I spoke to Fig first.

"Watch the guards," I said. "They can't be trusted." Which had me glancing around as I remembered the uncle I'd asked her to watch. "Where's Racheff?"

"Back in the library," Fig said. "I'm on it."

I had to believe that was true. If only for my peace of mind. I then turned to stride toward the one person who hadn't been corralled into containment, pretending my sister following me didn't only increase my sensation of being scored on my performance. If the guards were surprised I stopped to speak to Pim Ulpher, they didn't show it, likely assuming that I was merely uncovering every detail. Little did they know, I guess, just how close the victim's personal servant was to the situation.

"Matron," I said. "If you'll come with me, please."

Pim flinched but nodded immediately. The fact she hadn't run said either she had nothing to do with Theringale's death or she had nerves of steel and was an excellent actress. Either way, I honestly suspected her less and her son more and didn't relish asking the questions I wanted to ask in front of the household guard.

Just in case gossip hadn't spread and I could protect her from it if what Yarra said wasn't true.

Pim followed me as I pretended to know where I was going, though she quickly took the lead and guided me past the sweeping staircase and to a small, narrow door hidden in the façade of the painting. I found myself in a passageway that smelled of cooking food and realized she'd escorted me to the entry to the servant's area, likely on the way to the kitchen.

"This will do," I said. Pim paused, staring at the floor, hands clasped in front of her, lips trembling. "Matron, I have to ask you about your son."

She looked up immediately. "Ferrick had nothing to do with this," she said.

"So I was informed already," I said. "I understand he's been receiving training from a master rogue working here in Vorentine?"

Pim seemed startled, but not surprised, more so that I knew anything about it. Which had me annoyed with Mellie all over again.

"I don't know what you mean," she said, glancing at my sister who didn't say a word. Why then did the matron flinch again? Likely because Posh could say so very much without opening her mouth. Trust me, as a child I'd been unable to keep anything from her despite trying to. My sister's steady attention could make anyone confess to anything.

Which was why she should have been in charge of the investigation, but I digress. Besides, maybe that confession thing just worked on little sisters who wanted their bigger, smarter, prettier, older sibling to like them.

And just like that, my family history was showing. Wait, what? It already was?

Oh, hush.

"Tell me about your master," I said, changing direction. I'd be getting what I needed about the boy from Mellie anyway, and I could circle back around when I had Pim more at ease. If that ever happened.

The woman's frown ended in a nod. "Master Balmont's passing was… unusual," she said, barely hiding her sorrow. Could she make it more obvious that she'd had feelings for him? The possibility that her son was the dead man's progeny only increased in likelihood. "It was fast and quiet and unexpected." She stiffened. "I won't gossip about this family, Master Bard. No matter what you do to me." Pim's gaze flickered to my sister again. "What either of you do."

"I don't know what you've heard about the Guild," I said with wry amusement I couldn't stop, "but we're not in the habit of torturing information out of anyone." I glanced at Posh whose flat, empty stare made her look like a threatening statue. And now I wasn't so sure if I'd lied to Pim or not.

The Master Rogue was my sister and even I was afraid of that face.

"I have to tell you," I said in a softer tone, leaning into Posh's choice to not only be silent but intimidating as she loomed there like a deadly statue ready to pounce on a moment's notice, "but there's been a suggestion of impropriety, Matron Ulpher, involving you and Master Balmont." Yes, I used sympathy in my voice but paired it with the leap I'd made.

Two things happened. Posh pivoted next to me, her tension radiating toward me as though to protect me from something I hadn't as yet recognized as a threat. And second, Pim flinched.

Trust me when I say that if whatever was about to happen made my sister react, it not only involved imminent danger, the source was about to be crushed underfoot and taken apart at the same time in fluid and effortless precision. Which meant I didn't have to react at all, trusting that she could handle whatever was to come with the utter faith and lack of fear that came from having Posh Yestervere as my sibling.

Pim's flicker of anxious acknowledgment was sufficient. That was all I got, though, in that instant of her reaction and my sister's.

But instead of the attack that Posh's protectiveness precursored, I instead heard a voice interrupt.

"Leave my mother alone," Ferrick Ulpher said, stepping out of the shadows with Mellie behind him. "She didn't hurt anyone."

# CHAPTER SEVENTEEN

Posh didn't say a word, leaving the young man to me, true to her decision to give me the lead on this case despite the fact she had way more experience with this sort of thing.

Having Mellie on one side and my talented and impressive sister on the other wasn't helping, but I managed to focus on Ferrick anyway.

"Nice to finally meet you," I said with the dry tone that I'd picked up from dealing with troublesome audience members, not quite snarky but definitively sarcastic. "Ferrick Ulpher, I presume."

He nodded to me, the slim young man almost tripping over his own feet as he took another step closer. It was clear that his sense of self-preservation warred with his need to protect his mother, the anxiety on his plain and earnest face triggering my empathy despite my suspicions about his reason for following the victim to her home.

"I am," he said while Mellie sighed visibly—if silently—behind him, her gaze locked on my sister.

"Might I ask," Posh spoke up, "what your business is here, Master Rogue Savos?" I'd mentioned Mellie to my sister, but the way she addressed the unhappy fellow in her order had me wondering if the two had met at some point in the past and, if so, what history might have triggered Posh's flat and unfriendly question.

Well, it wasn't a stretch to assume they knew one another. But was I imagining Mellie's distance and discomfort or were they both a bit too cold with one another for comfort?

"Queen's Rogue," Mellie said in that same nothing voice Posh had used. "I'm merely here as an observer."

That huge lie wasn't going to cut it. "Since I've personally witnessed this young man," I said, "stalking the Vorentine family while you," I jabbed a finger at her, refusing to protect her when she clearly had more to do with this situation than was healthy for her, "intcracted with young master Ulpher, I'm calling foul, Mellie."

Her lips pursed briefly, gray eyes angry as they flickered to me. What, did she think I'd side with her against my own sister? She had far too high an estimation of herself if she believed that for a second.

"Ferrick Ulpher is innocent of the murder of

Theringale Vorentine," Mellie said like that was the end of the conversation.

"If you're claiming to be his alibi," I said, "you can explain why it is I personally witnessed him creeping around outside the house prior to her death." Mellie grit her teeth while Ferrick turned very red, his embarrassment doing nothing for his case. "Are you telling me you simply followed him around while his incompetent attempt at whatever it was he planned unfolded?"

She didn't answer.

Posh did, though. "As a Master Rogue of good standing in the Guild," she said, "I do expect that you didn't attempt to offer instruction to a young man who failed out of our academy." Wait, he'd what? My sister gestured, a faint red sigil appearing over Ferrick's forehead, the Rogue badge emblem burning briefly before vanishing.

"I'm aware," Mellie snapped back. "Queen's Rogue Yestervere."

Definitely some kind of history there. Did I want to know?

"It was my idea," Ferrick blurted. "I recognized her from the academy. So when I spotted her in the street, I approached her and begged her to train me."

There was one hundred percent more to it than that because no way would Mellie get herself involved with a mess like this one without very good reason. Her face contorted a little as he confessed, but she didn't argue.

"I said no," Mellie finally said when he stopped

talking and left the silence to grow awkward. Why was it I didn't entirely believe her? Her time under deep cover had left her outside the normal confines of Guild law. I'd learned that from experience. Was she going to be a problem?

"Leave my son alone," Pim said abruptly, terror on her face but determination there, too. "Ferrick, I told you to go."

"I couldn't let them accuse you, Mother," he said in a voice vibrating with worry. "Think what you want of me, but my mother didn't hurt that horrible woman."

I wasn't going to tell them that their attempts to be one another's character witness in this situation weren't helping. "Young sir, why were you following Theringale Vorentine?"

"I wasn't," he said, sullen enough his lie only made me angry.

"Your next words better be truth," I said, snapping in irritation, "or I don't care if you did the deed or not, you'll be facing the inside of a cell for lying to a Guild investigator."

He glanced at Mellie. Which only fired up my temper even more. She nodded to him before he shrugged and sagged in place.

"Balmont Vorentine was my father," he said. Pim paled as her whole being seemed to compress in response. "I just wanted Theringale to admit it." His head lifted, eyes meeting mine, simple honesty far more believable than his sullenness had been. "She wouldn't talk to me," he said. "I didn't find out until it was too late who he was." Pim flinched. So, she'd kept it from her son until after Balmont died? Interesting. "Theringale had me thrown out the one time I came to see her directly. So, I've been following her, trying to find a good moment to speak to her privately, alone." He scowled then, shaking his head as he looked down, frustration undisguised. "She's *never* alone," he grumbled."

He used present tense. In my (notably thin) experience, that usually indicated the person speaking still thought of the victim as an adversary or someone to confront. And often implied no connection to the death, since unfinished business remained.

Not that such things were evidence or anything. Whatever the case, it was time to take Ferrick and his mother elsewhere that they could be separated and questioned without the other's influence.

"Both of you," I said, gesturing at Mellie who nodded, if grudgingly, "come with us." I turned like I knew what I was doing, Posh pausing as I led the way. I knew my sister would be in last position, watching everyone with her focused attention, and trusted that she had my back.

Though, as I passed through the door and into the foyer again, I did glance back, noting that my sister and Mellie were exchanging a heated whispered conversation, short and angry, that had me wondering what I was missing and if I should make a point of finding out.

After the murder investigation, I guess. And more to the moment, before Justes Vorentine added a corpse to the body count. Because despite my instructions, Fig had clearly lost control of the scene and, with a shriek of rage, the heir to the Vorentine business holdings had already launched himself toward me, his furious gaze locked on someone over my shoulder.

One guess who it was his extended blade was aiming for.

## CHAPTER EIGHTEEN

Posh was, as always, faster than I could ever have been and had the young heir pinned and under control before I inhaled to tell him to stop. My sister looked up from what amounted to hog-tying Justes with a short length of leather from her belt meant as just such a restraint without batting an eyelash, nodding to me in her efficient and casual way.

Once again reminding me why it was she had the reputation she did and that despite my parents' faith in me, I was the wrong person to be running the show.

That being said, I was fast enough to nab Darmilla as the now groaning young man's wife tried to reach him. It surprised me that she cared enough to try to defend him, though the fury on her face aimed at Ferrick had to have had something to do with it.

"Imposter!" She fought against me, not even close

to strong enough to break loose. I might have been a bard, yes, but years on the road meant a certain level of agility, athleticism and core strength, not to mention my elf heritage lending me the advantage over the small human woman who struggled against me. We elves might have appeared all frail and willowy (some of us, that was) but whether magic or simple evolution, pound for pound we could take out most opponents twice our size with relative ease.

That didn't mean I couldn't feel it when her teeth dug into my wrist, though Mellie quickly divested me of the wriggling and angry bride of Vorentine. I didn't show my discomfort (while humming a bar of music to the spot to make sure she hadn't infected me with something), embarrassed that my business had been handled twice now.

Fig appeared from behind Racheff, the towering uncle of the family scowling at me while my friend's pale green eyes warned me of what was to come.

"You!" Racheff's big hand reached for his waist on clear instinct, though he wasn't wearing a sword and his fingers instead closed on empty air. He spun with a tsking sound, snapping his fingers at one of the guards for a weapon.

"Enough," I said. Racheff spun back, furious to be ordered around at a time like this, only to back off when I flashed my teeth in my own grimace of anger. "I said, enough!"

He stilled, though I could tell if I didn't get things under control quickly, he'd be back in motion, this time armed and dangerous, with Ferrick Ulpher as his target.

"What is that *person*," Yarra's biting tone barely hid her delight at this new tidbit to titillate her, "doing here?"

"My son," Pim spoke up, voice shaking but her shoulders back, "is here to claim his birthright."

"You're a liar," Justes said, though any attempt he made to move was quietly and efficiently curtailed to the point that my sister barely seemed to hold him. "I want that fraud arrested for his lies." He blinked as though only then putting the pieces together. "And for the murder of my mother."

Ah, so it was Ferrick's claim of brotherhood that had Justes wound up, not Theringale's death?

"Until such time," I said, "as a healer can confirm or deny the paternal lineage of Ferrick Ulpher, he'll remain in protective custody. Anyone who makes any attempt to harm him will be dealt with severely." I let them all absorb that for a moment, only going on when Racheff finally nodded. "Posh, please release Master Vorentine."

She did so, slowly and with her signature liquid grace, easing up on him while Justes rose from the floor. But not of his own power, I assure you. Posh lifted him back to his feet and made sure he was secure on them—or as secure as could be expected—before she backed off herself. I had no doubt that he'd be once again on the ground and bound if he made one false move.

As for Darmilla, she shook Mellie off, the other rogue allowing it, though the gray-eyed undercover agent glared at me like she disapproved of my choices.

Let her. I just wanted this investigation over with, thank you.

"Fig," I turned to find my friend at my side, an apology on her face as she opened her mouth to speak. "I should never have left you alone," I said quietly, then raised my voice again. "Posh, Mellie," yes, I included the second rogue in the mix, if only to keep an eye on her, "please escort our suspects," Yarra had the temerity to gasp and clutch at her partially-gaping robe's bosom as though such a label was a surprise and insult, "back to confinement. And the next guard who lets even one of them walk free will answer to me."

The household soldiers didn't look happy, either. Which meant I was making friends all over the place. How awesome.

I followed Pim and Ferrick, noting that his mother reached out and took his hand before she turned to me. "Please, Master Bard," she said, tears trickling down her face. "It wasn't his fault. I should have told him everything. This is all on me."

"Mother," Ferrick said, deep hurt in his voice as he stared at her, pale and shaking. "I didn't kill Theringale."

Pim tried to reassure him, but I couldn't have been the only one who saw her hesitation. He didn't wait for her to speak, ignoring her outstretched hand, instead retreating without being prompted through a small doorway with a guard on his heels.

"Soldier," I snapped. The young woman turned back and met my eyes, hers huge. "He'd better be in the same condition when I return as he was when he went in."

She nodded quickly and closed the door behind her, but not before Fig shrugged and joined them, winking at me.

Perfect. But that had me turning to watch the guards again segregate the family while Posh and Mellie directed them, Racheff the last to disappear behind the library door. His glare across to me had to be tied to Ferrick's protection and while I had hoped the uncle might continue to support the attempt to find his sister's murderer, it was clear that any assistance was now smothered by the fact that he believed the culprit was none other than Ferrick Ulpher.

Mellie joined me, Posh slipping out the front door, more than likely to check in with her feralfolk companions. I stepped aside under the large staircase into the shadows, keeping an eye on the foyer while the rogue, who clearly wanted to talk, joined me.

"It's not what you think," she said.

"That Posh is right," I told her, "and you're training a reject from the academy against Guild rules?" I shook my head at her, raising one hand to silence her protests. "Whatever the case, there's more to this than you're telling me. Why am I not surprised by that?"

She bit her lower lip, that sensitive and vulnerable side of her surfacing. I'd begun to think it was an act meant to soften me up, but I couldn't tell and that troubled me more than anything. I hated being a sucker more than I disliked misjudging people.

"I was one of his trainers at the academy," she said in a soft voice, tsking when I inhaled to berate her. "He reminded me a lot of me, all right? I was only there for a week, just a short stint to fill in the gap between being undercover and returning to active duty." She looked away, face angry. "It's been… difficult." Well, she'd been out of regular action for years and had finally resolved a personal vendetta not so long ago, so I guess I could understand. "I didn't have any support either and almost got booted for insubordination in my first week." She glanced back over her shoulder at the open doorway, the implication clear. "The only reason I was allowed to stay…"

"Posh," I said. I didn't quite groan, but I might as well have.

Mellie shrugged. "We go way back," she said. "The point is, she gave me a second chance. When Ferrick was expelled for a minor infraction, I fought for him." Her bitter resentment was showing, whether she liked it or not. "I swear to you, I was just trying to help him."

"Do what?" I wanted to shake her. This was the second time we'd encountered one another over a dead body and though the first led me to wonder if she'd been a murderer herself, it had revealed the truth about her undercover work and her own personal demons. So, whether truth or fabrication, it tracked that she felt some affinity to the young man after her loss and vow of vengeance.

"I don't know," she said, huffing in anger she couldn't quite express, like she'd bound it tightly inside her, pale skin flushed pink with it. "One thing is true though," she said with a rueful grimace, "the kid is not suited to the job as things stand and there's a very good reason he washed out." She bit her lip as though saying so went against everything she wanted to believe. "At the time, that is." Way to try to defend him again. But if his terrible attempts at sneaking and skulking were any indication, she was just being kind and likely now taking on a position that wasn't going to end well.

"He might be your former student," I said, "but if he's a murderer, Mellie, I have to know."

"He had no reason to kill her," Mellie said then, her intensity returning. "If anything, doing Theringale in only makes it harder for him in the long run. He needed her to acknowledge him as Balmont's son in order to collect any inheritance." While children out of wedlock didn't always find soft places to land, Valorian law clearly stated that any blood of a line with inheritance at stake could petition for a portion of that fortune. So, if anything, Ferrick was the threat, not Theringale. Especially since he still had Justes to petition.

"Unless part of his plan was to kill the heir, too," I said, then again waved off her protest. "Fine, you say he didn't do it. Were you with him? Are you claiming to be his alibi?"

Mellie hesitated, licking her lips, before finally shaking her head. "I… was working a job," she said.

The real reason she'd been here in Vorentine, maybe? "An assignment." Not a good look, getting distracted like this. She'd been on her own too long. The Guild didn't take kindly to members who allowed personal matters to influence their cases. "When I heard what happened, I wrapped up my assignment and came immediately." She tossed her hands. "I should have been here for him."

"Not your task," Posh said. I jumped because she'd snuck up on me, though Mellie didn't seem surprised by my sister's appearance. Of course. Rogues, am I right? "In fact, I believe now that your assigned case is complete, you're due to return to the Guildhall for your next one."

Whatever she'd been here for was over, then? I looked back and forth between them as their silent battle of wills waged in utter nothingness, and it was Mellie who backed down first. Hey, I hardly blamed her. She might have been the lone wolf type, but not even she could stand against the wall of utter power that was my sister.

"I'd like to stay and assist," she said. To me, directly. That took courage. Not to mention putting me on the spot.

"Fine," I said. "But you need confirmation from the Guild in my hands right now or you're out."

Mellie bowed a little and spun, hurrying off toward the door to the drive, leaving me with my sister.

Who didn't watch her go like I did, instead watching me. Can you say disconcerting? I can, and did in my head before bracing myself for whatever was to come.

"She's talented," Posh said then in her soft, deep alto, "and brilliant. But the chip on her shoulder could crush a rock troll and she's had enough run-ins with the Guild to make her a target. Have caution, sister." With that, she stepped back. "The healer has arrived," she said with a little more volume. "I thought you'd prefer we waited for you to join us before he got started."

"Thanks," I said, striding past her, knowing she'd understand my gratitude was threefold. For the courtesy in the case, of course. For the warning, because yes. And for letting me make my own decisions while ensuring I had the information I needed.

And that, my friend, was why everyone loved Posh.

Me included.

# CHAPTER NINETEEN

I stood outside the carriage, the cleric healer floating the body out and to the paving stones, settling the remains of Theringale Vorentine gently on a sheet he'd spread for that purpose.

"Not ideal," Malim Thistleweave muttered, the gnome's bald head shining in the light generated by the staff he carried. "But will have to do. There, the cause of death." Obvious enough of course, and one I'd already identified. "You know as much," the small cleric grunted. "Let's see if we can find any magic, too." He breathed over the body, a cascade of golden sparkles raining down on Theringale, only to die out as soon as they touched her. When he finally looked up, brown eyes meeting mine, he shook his head. "No power touched her in her last moment of death," he said.

"Can you please remove the poniard, healer," I said. "I need to examine the weapon for clues."

He nodded, bending down, humming softly as his hand, sheathed in more golden light, grasped the hilt, his magic creating a barrier that prevented his touch from damaging any evidence. It slid easily free, the long, pointed blade clean as it exited, settling on the sheet next to the widow's body.

I crouched with Posh at my side, the pair of feralfolk both sniffing over my shoulder.

"Lans," she said, "if you would?"

"My pleasure," the hare-like twin said, thumping one back foot into the ground, the vibration traveling through my bones. His magic flared around the hilt, but when I tensed in anticipation of seeing an imprint of the killer holding it, I was disappointed.

I'd already guessed whoever used it had hidden their identity. Otherwise, why leave the weapon behind?

"Me next," Lire said, flashing me a foxy grin as she shook her head, her pointed ears perked. When she let out a yipping whine, the blade blossomed with magic this time, humming as it bounced gently on the sheet. I thought perhaps she'd managed it, only to see the vague outline of the cleric appear before vanishing again.

"Well," he huffed at her, "I certainly didn't kill Madam Vorentine."

"No one thinks you did, Healer Thistleweave," I reassured him. "Posh?"

My sister shook her head. "I have nothing the twins couldn't manage," she said. "Rogue power has done this." She met my eyes, hers carefully empty. "It's the only explanation as to why our magic can't resurrect the wielder."

That was… interesting. And made sense. "Then maybe bard magic might do the job," I said, refocusing on the weapon in question. The song I chose was an old warning tune, a parody meant to teach children about the dangers of the Everwilding. It carried its own embedded magic, as ancient as the songsmith who'd made it, easy to piggyback my query onto.

Sweat broke out across my back and upper lip, my chest tightening as I came up against the erasure of the murderer's identity. Whoever wiped clean the history of the blade went back to its very founding, the heat of the smithy that forged it sizzling back along the edges of the song and scorching my tongue.

I sat back on my heels, shaking my head, sucking on the sore spots for a moment. "Looks like we're back to asking questions," I said.

Posh rested one hand on my shoulder, nodding to me. Wait, was that respect in her gaze? The slightly awed look from her feralfolk vanished as soon as I noticed it, so I likely just imagined their reaction, but even considering they might have been impressed helped to bolster my confidence.

"With gratitude, Healer Thistleweave," I said. "If you would take the body and do a thorough examination in case we've missed something, the Guild would appreciate your efforts."

He grunted and shrugged. "I'm not accustomed to taking orders from the Guild," he said. "But our Madam Vorentine deserves our very best. If I discover anything at all, I'll contact you forthwith." He gestured and the body wrapped itself in the sheet, the weapon included, binding around Theringale's corpse where it floated, bobbing softly under his magical support, as he turned and headed for the gate. I sent two guards with him as escort and, that part complete, focused on the carriage.

Lans and Lire had already repeated their actions while I remembered that Fig and I had come, not in this blue one, but the black that Theringale favored.

"Why was she even in this carriage?" I frowned as I asked that question out loud, then filled Posh in on the important bit. "This wasn't hers." When an image materialized, I thought perhaps the twins had done it, only to see Darmilla alighting from the interior, a guard taking her hand to steady her to the ground. Racheff appeared and hefted Justes out of it before all three disappeared in fading aftereffects of their lighted outlines losing power.

"That's it?" Posh accepted the mutual shrugs of her rogues before turning to me. "Again, rogue magic," she said. "Skillfully applied. I've never seen such lengths managed."

Wait, did my sister just admit she couldn't do something? Never mind that she hadn't once claimed, to my knowledge, to be perfect. I'd always just assumed.

Which had me singing a new song as I held out

one hand, letting the tune slide down my arm and through my fingertips to the doorway and the small, dark puddle on the carpet there.

This time, the song I chose was about love and loss and the broken heart of a yearning widow. I could have picked a battle anthem and forced my way through or even a dark and threatening nocturne to infiltrate anything remaining. Instead, I tried softness and sorrow and guilt and grief and, for the briefest of moments, felt myself connect.

And threw three more notes into the mix, swelling the refrain in volume and emotion, feeding the thread that the killer had missed.

It wasn't much. Barely a flicker of a figure, indistinct and unidentifiable. But when I finally had to give up the music, the last of the final note dying away, Posh clasped my shoulder with one hand so firmly I looked up.

Into her tear-filled eyes. "Beautiful," she said. "And more than anyone could have asked for. Well done, sister."

"It didn't work," I said, not sure why I needed to protest.

"Perhaps not," she said, "but you accomplished what others could not." Lans and Lire were grinning at me, the hare bouncing on his furry feet, his sister clapping her soft paws together. "I think your talents have grown from your days wandering the borderlands far greater than our parents could ever have imagined."

Okay, her sisterly pride was going to make me

burst into tears in a second. I had to lighten the mood, quite literally.

"Too bad Thune isn't here to smite it with Light," I said.

Posh laughed. "Perhaps Cloudest would be a better choice," she winked at me. "While I appreciate our brother's methods, his tendency toward blunt force has also shaped him in rather particular ways."

I grinned at her. Were we having a real-life sibling moment? And was I wishing Thune was there to share it? Wait, was I suddenly and inexplicably missing being a Yestervere?

What was wrong with me?

As Posh spoke to Lans and Lire, voices low and their privacy less cutting me out as much as it was a method they obviously cultivated through association, I found myself warm on the inside even as I fought off a wave of grief.

I'd missed so much, so many opportunities to get to know my siblings, all out of a need to make my own path, to make sure no one compared me to them. But what had I lost in that (let's be honest, ridiculous and childish) craving for independence?

And why was I now deciding that the time might be coming that I rectify that distance?

I didn't get to say anything to my sister about it, however, as she stiffened suddenly, head high, gaze lost in the distance while her deep blue eyes went dark. Lans and Lire froze in place, watching her intently until she nodded as though to whatever message she'd just received, the power contacting her retreating.

"Forgive me, Elora," she said with enough intensity that meant she was anxious, something rare for my sister. "There's something I need to deal with."

"I'll be fine," I said. "Go."

She hesitated. That said a lot and stirred my feelings all over again. "I'll be back," she said, stepping through the portal that appeared in a dull hum, the feralfolk slipping through at her back. Posh paused to hold my gaze as the portal flickered. "I have no doubt you'll have solved this by the time I return." And then, she vanished with the wavering light in a soft pop of dissipating magic.

I instantly missed her for all the right reasons. But I had a job to finish (even if I didn't need to earn her respect by doing so, imagine that?) and even more determination than ever.

# CHAPTER TWENTY

Dad reached out as I headed for Theringale's office with instructions from one of the servants.

*You asked about Racheff Sargot,* he sent. *The brother of your victim, I believe?*

*Dad,* I sent back, *you didn't have to contact me yourself.* He could have left that to message magic, even sent me a line of song. It wasn't like he didn't have the power to do so. In fact, he should have had a subordinate do it.

*I'm delighted to help,* he sent, his power embracing me. *Besides, things are quiet around here and your old dad craves adventure now and then.* The low hum of excitement in his touch had me grinning despite myself.

*Don't tell Mom,* I said. *She'll drag you out on the road again.* The very idea had me shaking my head. The world wouldn't survive a Yestervere return to adventure.

My father chuckled through his connection to me, warming me with that adoring magic we shared. *It would be so much fun though. You, your mother, me, your siblings. We'd be unstoppable.* Hey, he included me? Why did that give me a bit of a thrill? No time for ridiculous suggestions, thanks, especially after years of pushing back from any possibility of such an unlikelihood.

I didn't get to wonder why I felt a whisper of stirring enthusiasm. Dad sighed then. *Racheff.* His tone shifted to more stately. *He served in a small company for fifteen years, nothing really of note until his group encountered a rock troll in their last campaign. Tragic*, Dad paused then. *He was the only survivor, found by another company and rescued. He returned to Vorentine and has served his sister's merchant interests ever since.*

*Thanks, Dad*, I sent. So, Yarra told the truth. But it sounded like Racheff's sister Theringale gave him a place to land after his near-death. Could there be a reason he resented her for it?

*Love you, Elora.* His touch faded but never entirely went away, my father's power linked into the badge under my jacket. I tried not to think about it or leap to the conclusion that he and Mom were watching me. Which they were, of course.

That interaction paired with the intensity of my interaction with my sister only faded as I paced through the quiet halls of the house on my way to the matron's personal apartment. It wasn't lost on me that the close proximity with Posh and my enduring heroine worship of my amazing sibling was likely clouding my judgment. Now that I was on my own, in fact, the anxiety over losing my anonymity returned. Unless I could somehow disconnect Elora Yestervere, Guild Master Bard with Elora Tune, simple songstress, I was again on the precipice of being outed to the point that I could very much lose any ability I had to carry on with the life I'd built.

A life I still loved, of course. But as I pulled open the door to Theringale's suite, the black-lacquered entry the one the little maid informed me belonged to her, I heard that tiny voice in my head that often whispered to me when I wasn't expecting it asked a question that had me stopping to consider my answer.

Would it really be such a bad thing to give up this life and go home for a while?

There had been a time not so long ago that the response would have been a resounding yes, are you kidding me? Goddess and stars, don't make me. Except now, I wasn't so sure. But nor was I willing to go into it with myself and that little voice in my head just yet.

Case first. Life decisions later.

Something rustled as I entered and I froze in place when a figure jerked upright near the far wall next to the fireplace. Thankfully, despite the fact there was almost no light in the room, my night vision allowed me to decipher Racheff's presence before he could figure out who I was so when I summoned a small ball of glowing power with a whistled tune he was startled while I was merely irritated.

Even more so to find out he'd been rifling through his sister's safe.

"Mind telling me what you're doing?" I hadn't considered him high on the list of suspects, but this obvious activity now had me wondering. Was there some possibility he might inherit himself if his sibling passed away? The man was clearly talented when it came to weaponry, not to mention knowing where to stab someone to end them quickly and quietly. Then again, I hadn't detected magic on him, the idea of a fighter of his bulk and stature managing rogue magic laughable. So how had he managed to eliminate any trace of himself?

Did he have a partner in crime I hadn't considered and could her name be Yarra Astir?

Racheff's visible frustration turned to sullen acceptance as he backed away from the open safe. I wasn't anticipating a physical attack, though the chance of it was high. If anything, he seemed defeated, ready to give himself up, that attitude refined when Fig came huffing through the doorway with a guard behind her.

"Racheff is—" Clearly, she'd been about to inform me of exactly what I already knew, her concern now flaring into fury. "How?" My poor friend was at her wit's end, no doubt about it, her words almost lashing him as she stomped one foot in irritation. "I had one job," she muttered.

"There's a secret exit through the bookshelf," he shrugged. Which he knew about, naturally.

"Leading right here, to Theringale's quarters," I

said without a trace of surprise and, might I say, leaning heavily into my sister's pitch-perfect flat and empty tone. He'd had a great deal of time between returning there and now, if I recalled correctly, so why was he still here?

Racheff didn't respond to that statement to the affirmative because it wasn't necessary. "It doesn't matter anymore," he said, sinking into a chair, head down.

"It does," I said, crossing to the safe, noting that he'd ignored the piles of gold, the small velvet bags that no doubt held precious gems or jewelry. "What document did you seek, Racheff?" Because the only thing disturbed? The sheaf of parchment piled at the bottom, looking rifled through and disorganized.

Nothing about Theringale Vorentine struck me as either.

"Her ledger," he said, spreading his hands. "It's not there. I looked everywhere."

And now I knew why he lingered long enough to get caught.

"Who sent you for it?" If he had a head for accounting, I was a goblingahst. And since I didn't live in an underground cavern feeding off the dead...

Racheff shook his head, face now stern. "Are you going to arrest me?"

"For breaking into your sister's safe?" I shrugged, crossing my arms over my chest. "Or conspiring to kill her?"

He sat up straighter, spluttering because I had his attention at last. "I didn't," he said.

"She took you in," I said. "After your rescue from the Everwilding." He flinched but nodded. "She gave you a position in her household."

"Theringale was good to me after my company's passing," Racheff said in a dull voice that suggested otherwise. "I was grateful."

"Were you," I said. "And she didn't hold your failure over your head or anything."

He shrugged. "I did fail," Racheff told me, old hurt and shame vibrating in his voice before he pulled himself together. "Any harsh treatment was well deserved."

Hmmm. "So, she browbeat you into doing what she wanted and forced you to be grateful. Anyone would resent her for it." He didn't comment. "Fifteen years of that weighs on a man," I went on. "Especially a proud one who never recovered from the loss of his company."

"It was my fault," he said, voice dangerously soft. "I triggered the trap that alerted the rock troll to our presence. It was an amateur move and it got everyone else killed. They should have left me there to die, too."

Shame was a horrible and debilitating emotion. I glanced at Fig whose expression clearly judged Racheff. I had other concerns.

"You took her insults all this time," I said. "But did she finally go too far?" He twitched while I pressed him. "Maybe she got what she deserved at last?" I wasn't going easy on him, bludgeoning when perhaps I should have used a softer touch. Patience was a virtue and apparently mine had run out. "Did you plan to murder your nephew, too?" I let that sink in for a moment. "His bride? Where would the killing end?"

Racheff's distress only grew. "You have it all wrong," he said.

"Do I." I gestured at the safe. "Am I going to find something in there to the contrary? Perhaps a will that gives you everything when the family is gone?"

He spluttered but didn't deny it. "You think very little of me, Master Bard," he said then, quiet and hurt. "As little as I think of myself. My sister's judgment of me was well deserved. But yes, I was tired of how she treated me." His sudden shift to quiet pride was surprising. "It had only increased since Balmont's death. I had made plans to leave." He hesitated then, clearly with more to tell, though he stopped himself and finished with another thought. "My sister's estate has nothing to do with me. The only person who would benefit from Theringale's death was Justes."

So he said. Why did I believe him? "Not even her daughter-in-law?" What kind of monster was the mistress of Vorentine?

"Theringale protected Justes even when he found out about the betrothal," he said. "When he demanded his father reverse it."

When was that? "I take it that was the only way Justes agreed to go through with it?"

"Balmont insisted," Racheff said. "Theringale took steps. The children were unhappy. But it was an agreement with binding power, nonetheless."

Sad and usually more indicative of royals than commoners but who was I to judge? "None of which explains why you're here," I said, "aside from looking for some way to benefit from your sister's death, that is."

The change of topic back to him seemed to rattle his anger back to defensiveness. "We'd never—"

We. I knew it. "Who are you working with, Racheff," I asked, "and what are you up to?"

He didn't respond, lips tight. Well, he could just protect his little co-conspirator while I confronted the one I suspected directly.

"Bring him," I said to Fig who approached him with enough menace even the big ex-adventurer appeared concerned. "Gently," I told her.

"If you say so," she snarled, hand on her sword at her side. She was a third of his size, but furious and no one angered my gnome friend and got away with it. "Up and out, Racheff. Now."

He did as he was told, following me as I returned the way I'd come, sealing the suite door with a few hummed bars before returning to the foyer and, to his surprise, the library. I quickly secreted him and Fig behind the bookcase, jabbing a finger up at him.

"Say a word," I said, "and Fig will make sure it's your last."

She shot me a tight, furious grin that had nothing of amusement in it. Racheff nodded and stood quiet while I closed the shelving behind them and then had a guard bring me Yarra Astir.

The woman in question swept into the room like a damsel in distress, though her tears had finally dried up more than likely out of her weariness over mustering them. I gestured for her to sit, making sure she had her back to the bookshelf where Racheff waited before addressing her.

"I have my suspicions about Theringale's brother," I told her, using a conspiratorial tone and leaning close. She took the bait, eyes dancing as she, too, sat forward, nodding.

"Racheff," she snorted. "You looked into him, as I suggested?"

I nodded. "Your information was accurate. He caused the death of his full company."

"I told you," she said. "Theringale was such a good soul to take him in after that. She didn't have to, you know." Her exhale suggested she thought the idea a foolish one. I wondered how Fig was getting along with her charge behind the secret door? Had I made the wrong leap? "Theringale suspected he had his hands in her treasury but could never prove it."

Something thudded heavily, making Yarra jump but instead of letting it break our rapport, I spoke again. Because that sound confirmed everything I guessed, hadn't it?

"Interesting," I said. "Especially considering I caught him just a short time ago pillaging her safe."

Yarra's eyes flew wide, hand over her heart. "How horrendous," she said. "However did he find the combination to the lock?"

"How indeed," I said. "No doubt he watched her while she was opening it, secreting himself in her quarters somehow to do it. Or magic." I watched Yarra's face carefully as I spoke, catching her eyebrow rise and fall, her bated breath at certain words, and had my answer. "Likely by sneaking through the secret passageway in this very library that ends in Theringale's suite."

Yarra was onto me, I knew it the moment she realized what I was doing. Honestly, I thought her far brighter and that I wouldn't make it this far, so the fact that she gave me what I needed before sitting back and clamping her lips together, half-turning as though to look behind her before fixing me with a glare almost made me smile.

"What is this?" She huffed and squirmed, rustling the hem of her robe as though trying to reset herself. "My poor dear friend is dead and her brother is to blame and you're prattling about something I know nothing about."

Again with the heavy thump and this time, Fig was unable to stop Racheff from shoving aside the case and bursting into the library. From the hurt and broken expression on his face, the betrayal ran far deeper than I'd thought.

She'd just shattered his heart, hadn't she?

"I didn't kill Theringale," he said, voice strangled.

"Racheff!" Her faked attempt at surprise wasn't fooling anyone. "Wherever did you—"

"Oh, please," I sighed, rubbing my temples, a headache starting and likely only to get worse if she didn't stop with the ridiculous innocence act.

Yarra's head snapped around, eyes narrowing. "I didn't kill her either," she said. "But Racheff could have. He's a soldier. Did all kinds of adventures back in the day."

His face twisted, his hurt turning to bitterness and resentment. "Yarra was stealing from Theringale," he said. "She convinced me to help her hide the proceeds. We were going to take it and run away together." Racheff's anger faltered as he realized what he'd done. "I believed you when you said you loved me." That betrayal hit him deeply. Had she used his vulnerability against him? She must have. "I trusted you." Violence rose in his eyes, the visage of a man who'd ridden the edge of shame too long looking the truth in the face at last not a pretty thing to confront.

"Oh, pish tosh," she said to me, ignoring him completely. She had no idea how close she was to her own death at his hands. I'd seen his kind of teetering precipice break before and tensed, knowing I might need to take him down before he could kill her in blind rage. "He threatened me. Told me if I didn't help him that he'd kill me." Her cheeks turned very pink, new tears welling, panic making her chest heave.

She really committed to her lies, I'd give her that.

"Whatever," I said, standing up and gesturing to Fig who circled around to focus on Yarra with a vicious smile while I firmly placed myself between her and Racheff. "Where did you stash the money?"

"In the blue carriage," Racheff said in a dead voice. I'd misjudged his fury, saw it distill and collect inside him, controlled far better than expected. Instead of falling headfirst into a berzerker breakout, he seemed to be using it as fuel. Which more dangerous? "Where Theringale died."

Now, wasn't that interesting?

Except now Yarra was on her feet, babbling and visibly terrified, though it was real this time, I could feel the fear coming off her in waves. "I didn't kill her! Yes, I hated her." Her face contorted as she backed away from me and Fig, hugging her robe to her. "*I* was supposed to marry Balmont!" Her shriek of rage made Racheff growl an animal-like reaction. "He was supposed to be mine, not hers. She stabbed me in the back!"

"Which is why you stabbed her in return?" I cut through her tirade without pity and Posh's favorite steady coldness which made Yarra stop in her tracks and stare at me.

Her lips flapped a moment before she lunged toward me, Fig blocking her, though I knew she wasn't attacking. Yarra fell to her knees in front of my gnome friend, clutching at her.

"I swear," she said, "I didn't. Don't you see? It was so much more satisfying to undermine her all this time." Evil shone in her eyes now, finally visible. "To take from her that which she stole from me in the first place. I slept in her bed beside Balmont far more often than she did." She barked a little laugh that had my stomach churning. "All those times she was out, doing business." She didn't even look at Racheff, so she missed the hate that her betrayal sent him down into, his face a mask of death. "I didn't need to kill her. I had what I wanted." She licked her lips. "I moved the gold." She glanced at Racheff finally, though if fear of him hit her, she didn't show it. Maybe she couldn't see it through her own haze of horrible. "I took it and switched carriages to Theringale's. I was going to take the black one just to make her furious."

"Which means you were near the blue carriage," I said, though she was already shaking her head.

"I grabbed the box when I heard someone coming," she said. "It was the driver coming to tack up the horses. Ask him! He saw me. It was still in the carriage house when I retrieved the gold."

There was one way to check into all of this that had nothing to do with her story, though I'd be tracking that, too. With a little hum of a tune, I tested her for magic.

And came up with nothing. Yes, if she was a rogue, there was a chance she could have hidden her power from me. But even that would have left a weird kind of emptiness as trace. Instead, I confirmed that Yarra Astir was a terrible human woman with a black heart filled with hate and the need for retribution.

Not a trace of magic, though. Which possibly cleared her and while I wasn't totally sold, I was leaning toward guilty of the things she'd confessed to but holding off on naming her as the murderer just yet.

## CHAPTER TWENTY-ONE

With Fig off to retrieve the stolen gold from Theringale's black carriage, I had the guards escort Yarra back into segregation while using magic to ensure that Racheff couldn't use his little escape hatch again.

Not that he looked like he planned to do much more than sit in vibrating and sullen silence staring at nothing. Whatever he had planned, Yarra had better watch her step from then on. He'd been on the edge of breaking for so long, it was clear he'd been desperate to believe in something and someone. Yarra had successfully led him astray from the cruelty of his sister and his own mind, craving anything to believe in. To find out that someone you thought loved you back might have led to murder and betrayal was very likely breaking him inside where no one could see it.

Until it broke out and wreaked whatever havoc brewed. I felt for him, but his actions and history weren't something I could help him with. That journey either out of the dark or deeper into it was on him. All I could do was keep him under wraps so if he did break, it didn't end in another death.

Never mind the whisper in my mind suggested Yarra Astir deserved it, because that was beneath me.

"Keep an eye on him," I said to the guard. "For real this time."

The soldier nodded though I wasn't holding my breath. I needed Posh and her team back to even the odds. Whatever had lured my sister away must have been important, however, and I couldn't begrudge her such a departure.

I had to risk it, heading back to Theringale's suite to investigate the safe. At least my power hadn't been tampered with or challenged, the seal on the door still there and only when I entered did I realize perhaps there was more than one secret entrance I should have been warding against. But if that was true (an oversight Posh would never know about), no one had taken advantage of it.

Which meant that the safe remained as I'd left it and I exhaled a short sigh of relief that my lack of foresight hadn't made things worse. With little time to examine it before the next drama unfolded (precedence, people), I dug through the paperwork.

Racheff hadn't had enough time to go through it all, apparently, and some had been shoved to the back of the deep hiding place. I paged through each sheet of parchment, only stumbling on the very ledger he'd been looking for when I dropped a page on the floor and had to retrieve it from where it floated under the bed.

Not the best of hiding spots, but had been more than enough to styme Racheff, so perhaps better than I believed it to be.

Reading through it, I found something else of interest that had me pausing. Not the entries themselves, however. I peeked at the ledger but without any context and no head for numbers, I didn't know what I was looking for. It was, instead, a piece of correspondence that caught my attention. The envelope was open, the seal broken, addressed to Theringale herself. When I unfolded the page inside and scanned the contents, I found myself scowling.

She knew about Ferrick before the young man could reveal himself and, in fact, from the date on the parchment, had known since Balmont's death. Let's be honest here, the woman was far from stupid. Surely, she'd been aware of her husband's penchant for dallying with other women? But this proved that she knew he'd fathered a child from one of those decisions, and as far as I could tell was the only one he laid claim to.

Because of Pim, perhaps? Or due to the fact that as far as he knew Ferrick was the only child he'd fathered out of wedlock?

The ledger itself would likely confirm what Racheff and Yarra had been up to, but was their activity even relevant at this point? I needed a bookkeeper to prove their thefts, though they'd already confessed as much. But could there be evidence in the financials of the family that revealed other heirs?

No, that made no sense. If Balmont was willing to admit to Ferrick—at least posthumously—then he surely would have shared if he had other children who he needed to be taken care of. Because the letter was very specific.

*I bequeath one-quarter of the inheritance of the estate*, it read, *to my son, Ferrick Ulpher*. From the sound of the letter, that money was meant to have been granted to Ferrick upon Balmont's death. That I could look for, and did, noting that no giant sum disappeared from the ledger a half year ago, nor did it seem as though Theringale made any attempt to follow through on her deceased husband's wishes.

More than wishes, I realized, the tantalizing touch of magic on the page remnants of the geas spell he'd had cast on it. Which meant that Theringale's refusal to do so must have left her in a great deal of pain. No wonder the woman was a grim and unhappy soul. Unfulfilled geases created a growing malaise that only increased with time. I winced as I considered just how far she'd gone to snub Ferrick and ensure that her own son inherited everything.

I wondered if she'd attempted to have the geas broken. No doubt. I didn't agree with Theringale's choice, but I had to admire her for her grit and mettle.

By the time I descended back to the foyer, it was

clear from the unhappy expressions on the guards' faces and the fact none of them would meet my eyes that the family had yet again bullied them into doing what they wanted rather than following my orders. Whatever. I heard raised voices coming from the salon and was about to barge inside, confronting the Vorentine contingent, when Fig came huffing toward me with a frown of her own.

"Yarra lied," she said when she came close enough to be heard at a bare whisper. "There's no stash in that carriage."

Or it was very possible that someone saw her stow it and stole it. A certain unhappy young thief with an axe to grind?

"Come with me," I said, striding past the nervous guards, not even bothering to give them a scowl, saving my disapproval for the family. Darmilla noticed me first, falling silent mid-shout, Yarra next and then Racheff. At least he hadn't murdered the obnoxious woman. In fact, he appeared to have pulled himself back from the brink of his rage, at least for now. Good for him.

We'd see how long it lasted.

Justes wavered on his feet, flipping one hand at me, making no effort to pretend he was regretful. To my surprise, Ferrick and Pim were with them, standing off to one side, the young man's body blocking his anxious mother. That saved me from having him brought here, at least. Silver linings and all that.

I held up the page, shaking it for attention. "Did any of you know that Theringale was geased to give a quarter of the Vorentine fortune to Ferrick and failed to do so?"

That stopped them all entirely, even Justes, whose face went ashen. I think he even sobered up somewhat at the news.

"No wonder madam was in such pain," Pim said in a soft, hurt voice.

Justes snarled softly, both hands cutting through the air as though severing him from any amount of care on the matter. "Irrelevant," he said.

"It's not," I told him. "The fact that Balmont willed the funds to your brother means that the magical seal makes it a legal and binding covenant, Justes."

"He's not my brother," the Vorentine heir snapped.

"I'm afraid he is," I said, handing him the letter. He almost didn't take it but finally did, the magic remaining in it sizzling over his fingertips as it did what I had expected it to.

Justes jerked at the contact, eyes huge and bulging as he stared at me. "The geas," he gasped.

"Now transferred to you," I said with a nod. "Your mother didn't fulfill it so it falls to you." Hey, don't judge me. He would have found it and touched it at some point, all unknowing. I just precipitated the event.

Justes collapsed backward into a chair, the parchment crumpling in his hand. "I'll die before I give that street urchin a copper," he said.

"Likely," I told him. "But first, you'll live with the

worst pain you've ever experienced, growing more intolerable by the day, until your heart gives out and you collapse and die." Yes, that was a cruel delivery. Yes, he deserved it. He had a brother, like it or not and I was suddenly and keenly appreciative of the fact that I'd been neglecting mine. Was I projecting my own regret? I'm not saying I wasn't.

"I don't understand," Ferrick said in a sick voice, his mother hugging him gently.

"Balmont always promised me he'd look after us," she told him. "This is proof he meant it." She broke down into tears, her son holding her gently, while the young thief met my eyes, his face crumpling in loss.

"I didn't come here for this," he said. "I just wanted Theringale to acknowledge me. And Mother." He hesitated, jaw jumping. "And to confront her," he said.

"Ferrick!" Pim clutched at him, her tears doing nothing to hide her surge of fear. "It doesn't matter now."

"It does," he said, meeting my eyes again with his chin high. "I believe that Theringale murdered her husband for his fortune," Ferrick said, "and to punish him for being unfaithful."

# CHAPTER TWENTY-TWO

The uproar was expected, though I did note that Yarra didn't seem particularly surprised by the accusation which meant the thought had crossed her mind, too.

"It's true," Pim said, her willingness to speak up now that her son had gaining attention. She'd regained some of her poise, though she still wept silently, wiping at her tears as she did. "I always suspected that madam had something to do with Balmont's untimely death. And don't tell me any of you didn't have the same thought."

"Lying witch," Justes said. Without any sort of heat in his words, however, and a desperate kind of despair.

I let them sort it out for a moment, backing away to confer with Fig. "You didn't mention the missing money," she said. "Holding that back for a reason?"

I was about to answer when Darmilla approached me, hesitating and glancing over her shoulder. Yarra and Racheff had gone silent, Justes sagging in his seat, while Ferrick held his mother and no one seemed prepared to break the horrible silence again.

That was, except for Darmilla.

"What can I do for you?" I kept my voice down because it was clear she didn't want anyone overhearing, though her approach in the full view of the family might have meant otherwise.

"Master Bard," she said, anxious expression making her look younger than I knew she was, "I..." she again glanced at her husband before looking down, voice a whisper. "Can I please talk to you in private?"

I led her out into the foyer while Fig stood guard over the others, drawing Darmilla away from the guards and under the shadow of the stairs. "You have something to add about Balmont's death?"

She shook her head, then shrugged, hands wringing in front of her before she forced them to smooth over the front of her crimson dress. "I don't know," she said, voice cracking as she met my eyes with hers welling tears. "I think... Master Bard, I think my husband might have..." she swallowed hard, shifting her feet, as though prepared to flee.

"You think he killed his father," I said.

"And his mother." She covered her mouth with both hands, eyes huge as she caught her breath, as though she could trap the words she'd just said behind her grasp but far too late. When she let her hands fall again, she was weeping but coherent. "Justes would never," she said before faltering one more time.

I wasn't falling for anyone's emotions anymore, even if that made me a cynic. "You married for money, Darmilla," I said.

She nodded instantly, catching my hand and then letting me go again just as quickly as if afraid the act was ill-advised. "I've made no secret of it," she said. "Theringale and Balmont made the arrangements with my family years ago and I followed through, even after my parents died and left me what little they had left." She shrugged, hugging herself. "It seemed like I didn't have a choice. Besides, they made such a great effort to ensure that I was taken care of. I couldn't argue with their reasoning and Justes makes no demands on me that I'm not able to fulfill."

How tragic. Yes, my empathy was now wide awake and prodding me to soften a little despite my resolve. "That's a practical way to look at living your life," I said.

She blinked at me, a bare smile making her full lips quiver. "Some of us are forced to accept that the Fates have better plans for us than we could have made ourselves," she said. Darmilla fished into her sleeve, pulling out a page of parchment that she'd folded carefully. When she handed it to me, it was my turn to hesitate, though a simple whistle of magic revealed it was only paper, nothing more.

"I found this," she said. "It came with the post. It's only reinforced my concern."

I unfolded it and read the missive. While my eyebrows climbed despite my resolve to keep them level. "You understand what this means," I said, looking up from the order.

She nodded, tears starting up again, face crumpling in worry. "I do," she said. "According to the letter, Justes requested an assassin's guild hit on his parents six months ago."

A request that had been denied, the guildmaster's refusal to accept the assignment outlined and explained. While assassinations were technically legal, hiring the guild to eliminate both of his parents without justification aside from his simple request was outside the guild's mandate. Since Justes presented no proof of wrongdoing or illegal activity on their part, merely asked for their end, he'd been turned down.

As it should be. "Six months ago," I said. "Around the time that Balmont died?"

"Shortly after we were married," she said, hiccupping a little past her tears, clearly fighting to stay coherent. Her delicate shrug told me she had no illusions about her influence on Justes' choice to have his parents killed.

"Who was this addressed to?" It clearly stated at the bottom of the message that this was a copy of the original long delivered.

"Theringale," Darmilla whispered. "It arrived this morning and when I realized her death was a murder, I opened it, thinking it might be important." She caught her breath, cheeks very red as she fought for air. "I had no idea it would reveal such a terrible truth."

"You could have kept this to yourself," I said. "Why didn't you?"

Darmilla flapped her hands in front of her skirt in sad little paddling motions, drowning in her anxiety, as though doing so might lend her some measure of control. "Whatever I thought of this arrangement, I liked Theringale," she said. "She was kind to me and made sure I learned all I needed to about the business. Against the day that Justes wasn't able to handle things for himself." In other words, her mother-in-law knew her son was a drunk and needed someone reliable to keep the family going. She'd chosen Darmilla.

Which had me asking one last question. "Now that she's gone," I said, "do you stand to inherit?" Racheff said no, but was that true?

"Nothing," Darmilla said, shoulders back and chin rising, her distress unwavering but her pride still intact. "If my husband falls now, I will be destitute." She shrugged again. "More than likely, if Balmont did name his other son, illegitimate or not, that would mean Ferrick would have legal right inherit everything."

So convoluted, and yet I was getting a better picture now of what was at stake. "Thank you for sharing this," I said, holding up the parchment. "No one else knows about it?"

She shook her head, the soft, blonde curls framing her round cheeks bouncing. "I didn't tell anyone," she said.

I sensed magic rather than seeing it, looking up as Posh returned through the front door, the sound of the portal collapsing loud in the foyer. She'd landed just outside the doors this time, Lans and Lire right behind her and she headed directly for me at a ground-eating stride while I gestured for Darmilla to retreat.

She did so without escort, returning to the salon door, pausing to glance at me with her anxiety intact before going inside.

My sister nodded to me, gaze falling to the page in my hand before she met my eyes with her own raised eyebrow. "I take it I've missed some vital happenings."

"Your other case?" I didn't want to take her away from something more important, though I was relieved to have her back.

"An old issue," she said with a faint and distant frown, "that I'm still trying to resolve. The bits and pieces are plaguing me when they should be long done." Posh shrugged elegantly before tilting her head in curious patience.

I shared everything I could think of before handing off the parchment, my sister nodding over the page when I finished.

"One moment," she said. "I have an old adventure friend at the assassins guild who might be able to fast-track this for us." She bowed her head, suddenly surrounded in black mist before my tall and imposing sister flickered and seemed to vanish. Not invisible, no, not entirely, her stealth power shielding her from casual sight as she called up her magic.

It gave me the creeps and thrilled me at the same time, Posh's skill and talent were legendary and something I very rarely got to witness. I'd done so much in my life to avoid anything to do with engaging in full-on adventure that I realized I'd missed out on more than just my sister's company.

When she flickered back into full view, she handed me the letter, grim but pleased. "Confirmed," she said. "Aldos told me that the request was made by Theringale Vorentine and that this was sent directly to her from headquarters a fortnight ago."

So, she'd known about Justes' attempt for fourteen days and did nothing about it? My respect for her was only growing and though I would never approve of how she treated those beneath her, the fortitude it had taken for her to tolerate her son, the agony of the geas and her husband's betrayal... had she also known about Yarra and Racheff? I had to believe that was the case. And that Pim, her own matron, had a child by Balmont.

I don't think I could have endured what Theringale did without going full-bore ballistic on all of the above.

"Shall we ask young Master Vorentine a few pointed questions?" Posh grinned at me.

"After you," I said.

"Oh, no," my sister swept a bow, her elevated mood a bit of a surprise, "after *you*."

Whatever triggered her playful mood died off the moment Mellie appeared at the salon door, waiting for us.

"Watch her," Posh said, but not to me.

Why was I now anxious that Lans and Lire might take that order too far?

# CHAPTER TWENTY-THREE

Justes was still huddled in the chair where I'd seen him last when I entered the salon, though now Darmilla had put distance between herself and her husband, even if he hadn't noticed.

"Master Vorentine," I said, knowing that getting to the point was going to be necessary in his current condition, "we need to talk about this." I didn't hand over the order, but I did let him squint at it. It took him a moment to realize I was holding up a page in front of him and then to process what it said.

That had him sitting up straighter, guilt and distress crossing his face. When he spoke, it was the clearest he'd sounded since we'd first encountered one another so apparently all it took was me finding out he'd tried to kill his parents (and perhaps finally succeeded?) to sober him up.

"Where did you get that?" He reached for it but I held back, shaking my head. "I destroyed the only copy."

"Your mother had it sent from the guild's headquarters," I said. "Did you know she was aware of what you tried to do?"

"What's this?" Racheff's scowl aimed at his nephew, the old adventurer held out his hand for the parchment. I allowed it, if briefly, though that was all the time Racheff needed. He gave it back with horror on his face that quickly turned to rage. "You tried to have your parents assassinated?"

"You *didn't*." Even Yarra seemed shocked, and that was a first.

Justes sagged again, not looking up, while Ferrick supported his mother whose own reaction had her collapsing in despair.

"They denied the request," he said. "You already know that. I was drunk. I didn't mean it." His words and thoughts tumbled over one another as he fell into mumbling. "It doesn't mean anything. I didn't kill either of them."

"Racheff," I said, ignoring the young man's muttering, "is there any way Darmilla will inherit if her husband is found guilty of murder?"

The uncle glanced at her then shrugged, confused. "No," he said. "I already told you. She's not in the will and never has been. Neither am I, if you'll recall. I didn't lie about it." He didn't sound bitter this time, either. "The bloodline was all that Balmont cared about."

"Ferrick and Justes," I said.

Racheff nodded, now staring down at his nephew in distaste. "How *could* you?"

"They *made* me marry her," Justes shot back. "I didn't want to get married. I didn't want any of this. I just wanted to be left alone."

Darmilla's reaction told me she'd heard this before and wasn't freshly hurt by it, at least. "It's true," she said. "There was a contract, sealed with magic. Neither of us had a choice."

Justes pushed himself to his feet, swaying there, facing me down with more conviction than he'd shown all along. "I was glad when the guild turned me down," he said. "I didn't mean it and I dropped it immediately. Darmilla and I came to an… agreement."

She nodded to me. "We tolerate one another," she said with simple grace. "For the family."

And the wealth that meant? Fair enough.

Justes ignored her, as though struggling to comprehend. "How did Mother even know about the request?"

"More importantly," I said, "what was she going to do with it?" I didn't wait for him to answer because there was something I had to do first. "Watch him," I said to Fig. "Pim, with me." I turned and left the salon with her on my heels, my sister following, though I noted she left her companions behind.

Mellie grasped my wrist on the way out. "I'm coming with you," she said.

Why was she suddenly so intent? "Fine," I said,

then addressed Pim again. "Show me to Justes' quarters."

It didn't take a lot of digging to find what I was looking for. The black metal box filled with gold stuffed into the back of his closet under some clothes that reeked of alcohol surely wasn't meant to be there. I'd confirm with Yarra and Racheff that this was the container where they'd stowed their ill-gotten gains. But it was the small, blue bottle with a plain parchment label that had me frowning, the stopper holding in only a droplet of whatever substance had been inside.

I sniffed it and winced, the acrid scent making me uncomfortable, as much as the word inscribed on it: *Venilisk*.

"That's distilled basilisk venom," Posh said quietly. "Assassin's guild standard."

But they rejected the job.

"You might want to ask about Balmont Vorentine's symptoms," Mellie said, standing off behind me, arms crossed over her chest. She looked grim, angry. "I've had some experience with it in the past and it's been known to mimic heart failure."

"Sudden and fatal heart failure," Posh agreed. While her blue eyes locked on mine and she shook her head. Just a little.

Convenient, wasn't it, that his mother's stolen funds and the means that may have taken his father's life were both found so easily?

I turned to Mellie before Posh could, positive that we were both thinking the same thing.

"Tell me you didn't plant this evidence to clear

Ferrick's name," I said.

Her eyes widened, anger flaring there, before her jaw jumped and Mellie retreated. "So that's how little you think of me," she muttered. Before shooting rage at Posh, too. "And you."

My sister didn't comment, holding very still and quiet, though she radiated judgment, so unlike her that I had an epiphany moment that left me reeling.

"You two were a couple," I blurted. And now Fig's suggestion about Mellie and me was even more inappropriate.

They both flinched. Mellie, fine, whatever. But my implacable sister? Flinched. Posh's nostrils flared just a little, but she didn't deny it because she couldn't, could she?

"That's been over for some time now," my sibling said.

"Who's fault is that?" Mellie shot that at her, so heated I knew if I didn't come between them that we'd be getting very distracted very quickly.

"Whatever you two have to work out," I said, hands up and held out, the one with the bottle aimed at Posh, "if you can't handle it in this situation, step off. I mean it."

My sister backed down immediately. "What do you want to do?"

She meant about the case, of course. I spun back to Mellie who's sullen reaction wasn't nearly as impressive as Posh's. "Did you plant these?" I jabbed a finger at the box of money and shook the bottle.

"No," she snarled. "Thanks for asking."

"That means either Justes is an idiot," I said, which wasn't entirely unbelievable, "or someone is setting him up for murder." I sighed. "Someone with barely the rogue skills to pull it off and an obvious bent that got him kicked out of the academy."

Mellie looked like she wanted to argue but she shook her head instead and looked away.

"Let's go have another chat with the family, shall we?" I marched out, knowing Posh followed, Mellie beside her and did my best to give them some space. If that meant they wandered off to have it out on their own and in private, that had nothing to do with me, did it?

I was surprised to find they'd both remained in step with me all the way back to the salon. Which meant they'd put the case ahead of their personal issues. Well, they were trained rogues and emotions aside, they were of much more use to me not cutting each other to ribbons with words and blades.

Mellie had lugged the box of money, setting it on the low table in front of Justes, while I balanced the bottle on top. I watched Ferrick's expression from the corner of my eye, knowing Posh would be keeping a closer tab on the young man's reaction, but I didn't see anything that suggested guilt. Either he was a better actor than I thought (no, no, he wasn't) or he had nothing to do with the items in question.

And Justes really was that inept.

Except he took one look at the items and stood again, reaching behind him and holding something out to me. The leather-bound folder's flap was tied with a thong, stamped with the family crest. I took it, undoing the binding while Justes spoke in a dull and heavy voice.

"Father's will," he said. "I've had it all this time. Not even Mother knew." He shuddered, hugging himself, looking away. "It's going to come out, so it might as well be now. My brother," he spit that word into the quiet that fell, "was the elder." I quickly scanned the document and realized it was true. "That names Ferrick as the heir to everything." Justes dropped back into his seat. "I've known for years that I had a sibling. Knew about Pim." His fury and drinking problem now had a purpose, a cause. "I found it and replaced the will after Father died. Mother had no idea. But he told me, Father did. Told me everything a long time ago. And you wonder why I tried to have him killed." He snorted softly. "Whatever you think I did, I had no reason. The old will was with me, the new one would stand, only if Mother lived. Now that she's dead… I won't be hung for her murder. Or Father's." He slowly turned and glared at Ferrick whose horrified expression greeted his brother's back. "I'll give up every penny to make sure the real killer dies for what he did!"

Ferrick didn't speak, didn't argue. Instead, before even Posh could act, he pushed his mother away and snapped his fingers.

Vanishing into a wave of black that swallowed him whole before it cracked like thunder and disappeared.

## CHAPTER TWENTY-FOUR

I'd never heard my sister swear before. It was a remarkable thing, hearing the normally collected and stoic Posh Yestervere let loose a stream of increasingly shocking and abrasive words that crossed over into a variety of languages before landing back in Common with a rolling hiss of rage its finale.

Quite the performance. Though I had a moment as I realized that even my amazing and talented sister made mistakes. Maybe that should have made me feel better.

Instead, it only made me sad all over again because the pedestal I'd put her on had been part of the reason I'd run from who I was in the first place.

Way to come to such an understanding in the middle of another family's utter meltdown, Elora.

Mellie was the only one who seemed like she wasn't stunned by the young man's flight, turning and dashing from the room. Lans and Lire didn't hesitate, going after her, while Posh spun on me and grimaced.

"I'm sorry," she said. "I should have seen that coming."

She was apologizing to me? I'd botched this investigation, not her, underestimating the young thief who wanted to be more. It was clear now, however, that Ferrick was guilty and had fooled all of us.

Including his own mother. Pim's wide and terrified eyes told me as much.

"He couldn't have," she whispered. And broke down into horrible, bitter and anguished tears that he was no longer there to comfort her through.

"My brother," Justes said, his bitterness still burning as he leaned sideways and helped himself to a decanter of some amber liquid, popping out the stopper and drinking right from the crystal bottle, not even attempting to hide his drinking problem anymore. "I guess that means I get everything, then." He didn't perk, not even at that. "I hope it all burns to the ground."

"Master Vorentine," Pim said, barely managing to speak.

"Ah, Pim, dear," Justes said, wiping his mouth on the back of his hand, one leg now draping over the arm of his chair as he saluted her with the bottle. "Father did promise to look after you in his will. I'd be remiss if I didn't do as he asked."

"What are you doing?" Yarra's hiss held real

venom, the plump woman lunging toward him. "That's *my* money."

He squinted at her, grin tight and angry. "You," he said, "on the other hand, dear Yarra, can starve." Justes waggled his fingers at his uncle. "You, too. I hope you're very happy together."

"You have to do something!" Yarra spun on me. I wasn't sure what she thought I was capable of under the circumstances.

Justes laughed. "I'm revoking the Guild's permission to be in my city," he said, winking at me. "With thanks, of course."

That wasn't necessary, but I shrugged regardless. "I'm afraid my part in this is done anyway," I said. "Like it or not, Justes, the Guild will continue to pursue and apprehend Ferrick Ulpher and bring him to justice for the deaths of Balmont and Theringale Vorentine. But when it comes to family matters, that's outside my powers." I bowed a little to the young man who I was now positive would quickly and efficiently drink himself to death in short order, sad for him and his trembling wife. "Master Vorentine."

"Guild Master Bard Yestervere," he said in a grand voice. "You can show yourself out."

It only took moments to exit the house, to be escorted to the end of the drive, to wait as the clang of the metal gates signaled our not-so-polite expulsion from the Vorentine Estate.

Posh hugged me hard, letting me go only to grasp my upper arms in her hands and shake me just a little. "Not the ending we hoped for."

"But an ending," I said. "Thanks for the help."

"I'm going to track Mellie," Posh said, stepping away after hugging Fig, too. Her hands rose, black mist appearing around them, forming a kind of hood around her deep blue hair, shading her pale face, formed from the thin fabric that matched her cloak. "I have a feeling if anyone knows where our young Ferrick went, it's her." She shifted slightly, fading out as her stealth power kicked in. "I'll find you when it's done." And then, she was gone and I sighed at our parting.

I was going to miss her.

Fig and I had to walk back to the inn, my feet dragging, weariness washing over me as I noted the moon's heavy dip in the sky, almost gone behind the buildings of the city when we finally crossed the threshold at last and headed upstairs.

"Sleep," I told my gnome friend when she tried to talk to me. I pulled a pillow over my face, exhaustion winning, letting weariness claim me.

I didn't open my eyes again until sunlight forced me to, the covering I'd used fallen away when I'd rolled over. I blinked into the late morning rays, the height of the sun making me groan. So much for hitting the road early. At least Fig had left me to sleep, my friend gone from our room, though she had left me a note next to my guitar when I yawned and stretched and sat up to find it.

*Your boots are ready*, her tiny, neat writing said.

I looked down at the old ones, now sagging and propped against the hearth. They'd made it back to the inn, but the magic was now run out and I could see that I'd be hobbling my way to the cobblers for their replacements. Maybe I could wrangle Fig into picking them up for me and save myself the trip?

Except that would mean possible side trips on my friend's part and a long visit with pixies (she *loved* pixies) that would delay us even further. Groaning and pulling on the hateful boots that flapped unhappily as I donned them, I decided rather than walk the short distance, I'd let Pennywhistle do the toting.

After all, his shoes were new.

I didn't see anyone in the taproom as I slipped through, hearing voices in the kitchen and avoiding my hosts for the time being. I made it out into the courtyard and to the stable as stealthily as any rogue, which of course had me thinking about my sister again. Regret, Elora, really? I had lots of time. Elves were very long-lived and now that I'd grown up somewhat, maybe it was time to explore not only my relationships with my siblings but with my parents as well. And if an adventure or two happened along the way… was being a Yestervere such a hardship and calamity?

That question was going to have to wait. Because when I entered the stall that housed my horse, my mind elsewhere, I was very quickly dragged back to the present circumstances.

If only because the young man who waited for me there forced me to pay attention.

"I didn't kill my father," Ferrick said in a low and angry voice. "And I can prove it."

# CHAPTER TWENTY-FIVE

That was a big statement and had me nodding instead of the obvious reaction. "Okay," I said, "prove it."

He fumbled and stammered then finally caved. "Fine, I can't," he said, face hangdog and body tense as he sagged with his hands rising and falling in defeat. "All I have is my word."

That was anticlimactic. "Why did you run, Ferrick?" I reached out to Posh to alert her, noting a soft shimmer in the air and guessed she was already here.

"I knew I was being set up," he said.

"Your brother was the one with the evidence in his room," I reminded him, "not you." I watched the stealth shielding glide toward him past me, frowning a little as the straw beneath my sister's feet shifted. It wasn't like her to give herself away like that.

"No one would believe me over him," Ferrick said as Posh's mind touched mine.

*On my way*, she sent.

Which meant—

"I'll turn myself in," Ferrick said as Mellie—because of course, it was her—appeared behind him, arm around his neck, dagger to his throat.

"Yes," she hissed in his ear. "You will."

He froze, terror in his eyes, but he knew better than to struggle. "Mellie, I—"

"Shut up," she snarled through clenched teeth. "Don't say another word. I believed in you. I helped you. I'm such an idiot." Her gray gaze met mine. "I can make him disappear right here and now."

"Let him go," I told her, still not convinced he was the culprit despite everything. "Mellie, that's an order."

Yes, I outranked her. Yes, that irritated her to no end, though likely it was the circumstance that made her so angry and not the actual command. Whatever the case, the result was the same. Mellie swore softly and released him, just as Posh appeared at the stall door.

Bless my horse, the gelding nosing what remained of his hay as though uninterested in the drama unfolding beside him. It was a good thing Pennywhistle had such a solid set of smarts. I patted his neck in appreciation for his patience as my sister joined us, Lans and Lire hovering just outside.

"I didn't make it inside the house last night," Ferrick told me, ignoring both Mellie and Posh. He knew better than to gesture or make a single move, but he was intent on at least getting his story out. "Mother begged me not to do anything and, in the end, I realized it wasn't worth it."

Someone entered the stable, her high-pitched voice clearly identifiable. "I did it! Let him be, I killed Theringale and Balmont both!" Pim stopped between the feralfolk who watched her carefully as she clutched at the closed half-door of the stall, her dark gaze locked on me. "Please, let him go. I'm confessing to everything."

"Mother!" Ferrick did move then, trying to reach her, shaking his head and visibly distressed. "Don't do this."

Pim straightened, holding out her wrists, palms together. "Arrest me, Master Bard," she said. "I'm the one you want."

*Posh*, I sent.

*I'm sorry, sister*, my sibling told me with real regret, nodding to the twins. Lans hesitated, as disbelieving as I was, Lire shrugging and sliding a loop of leather around Pim's wrists. I did note the fox-faced rogue didn't pull it very tight, however, so she was as doubtful as her brother, but there wasn't much they could do about it.

"Pim Ulpher," Posh said in a sad voice, "are you certain you want to confess to two murders?" She let that hover a moment. "The penalty is hanging." Like Pim didn't know that already.

"My son is innocent," the matron said in a firm but shaking voice. "His life is just beginning. I will not see him killed for something he didn't do."

Mellie's fury snapped back and forth between mother and son. "You're going to let her do this?"

Ferrick seemed stunned and unable to respond, lips flapping but nothing coming out. The rogue tossed her hands and stepped off, shoulders rounding forward as if in defeat while my sister met my eyes.

*Tragic*, she sent, *but I'll do my best to speak for her at the tribunal.*

*She didn't do it*, I sent, frustration showing on my face, I was sure of it.

*I agree*, Posh sent. *However, a confession is all we have to go on and that is how the Guild operates.*

*Justes told us to leave*, I sent in a desperate attempt to stop this injustice.

*And yet, Pim Ulpher turned herself over to us*, Posh told me, already striding past me and out the half door of the stall. *All I can do is what I am mandated to do, Elora. What the Guild has assigned us both to do. If the real killer is found, Pim will go free.*

*Justes will never see the hangman*, I shot back.

*Sadly*, Posh sent, gesturing to her feralfolk who stepped back as she made a portal right there in the walk, just big enough for the four of them, *that is probably true. Forgive me, Elora, but this is what I must do.* This portal was less flashy and more efficient, proof that the ones used publicly were mostly for show. Not that I cared in the moment as my sister and her people stepped through, Pim between them, the matron glancing back with her dark eyes full of tears.

Ferrick did lunge then, trying to reach her, Mellie blocking him with a swift and violent move that brought him to his knees while the sucking snap of the portal took his  mother away.

"She didn't do it," he sobbed as he clutched his stomach, hunching in half in his grief.

"Then tell us who did," Mellie snarled back.

He looked up at her again, face torn between frustration and horror. "I don't know," he said. "I swear. Mother is going to die, Mellie. If I did it, don't you think I'd confess to save her?"

"I think," she snapped, turning her back on him and heading out of the stall, "you're a selfish little boy who doesn't care about anyone and I was a fool to even try to help you. He's all yours, Elora." And then, she was gone, the broken young man sobbing softly next to me.

# CHAPTER TWENTY-SIX

Ferrick left of his own accord, skulking away as I struggled to find some way to help. For the first time, I was truly convinced he didn't kill anyone. There was no way the grief pouring out of him wasn't genuine, though when he staggered to his feet and faced me, I could tell he wasn't quitting despite his collapse.

"I'll find out who did this," he said, voice shaking. "I'll save my mother, Master Bard. Or I'll confess and take her place." He stumbled away while I scowled after him, hating that the likely ending to this story was going to be a tragic one.

Justes Vorentine was going to get away with two murders. The more I thought about it, the more convinced I was that he'd set this entire thing up himself. Was he even as drunk as he seemed to be?

Had he arranged all of this, played a long game? Racheff had told me Justes had known about his upcoming marriage to Darmilla for years, so why on the eve of his wedding did he suddenly protest? Not to mention knowing about Ferrick and Pim well before he tried to have his parents assassinated. He had to have also understood that such a request would be turned down.

That had me leaning into Pennywhistle, stomach in knots. Was he, in fact, far more brilliant than I'd given him credit for? As I let the facts of the case wind together, I had to admit it was a distinct possibility. And now I felt very sick because what if Justes had planned all of this, setting himself up, knowing that it would look obvious and set up his half-brother to take the fall?

I couldn't shake the thought that I'd severely underestimated the young man because of his apparent alcohol addiction and stumbling buffoonery. He'd made a very public show of it, right from the moment we'd met at the gate and while I doubted he'd known who I was then, he'd made it very clearly known that he wasn't capable or competent and played the part of the dilettante perfectly.

The assassination order could be passed off as another ridiculous layer to his obvious lack of intelligence, though a risky one. What if the assassin's order had accepted the assignment? Then again, if they had, it would have been sanctioned without legal repercussions. Unless he really was drunk and stupid when he made the request, that was.

With orders to leave Vorentine by the ruling heir to the town's business consortium, I had no choice but to go or face action myself. Trust me, I considered it anyway. But while I leaned into my horse and debated the obvious, Posh reached out.

*Don't do it, sister,* she sent. Was she spying on my mind? More likely she knew what I was thinking, but it amounted to the same thing. *I don't want to have to arrest you next.*

*How can you live with this?* I threw that at her, like an accusation she didn't deserve.

*That's the job,* she sent back, sad but firm. *We follow the rules in the hope that justice prevails.*

*Hope failed this time,* I sent.

*It did,* she admitted. *But our hands are tied. Elora, please, listen to me. There will be a reckoning.* Wait, did she have something of her own in the works? *I need you to leave, now. Promise me.*

That did make me feel a little better, even if she couldn't just come out and say it. *Fine,* I shot back, though softer so she'd know I understood. *This is why I don't work for the Guild.* I hadn't meant to add that or the judgment that came with it.

*I know,* she sent so softly that I almost missed it. *You've always been the sweetest of us, Elora, the one who cared so much. Don't change, not ever. Even if that means keeping your distance.* My sister's mind embraced mine before she shut herself off.

Why was I crying? Allergies, that was it. The dust from the straw, I swear.

I still needed my stupid boots. Argh.

Pennywhistle seemed eager to get out on the road, carrying me quickly to my destination, while inside I argued with myself over just leaving town and doing nothing about the miscarriage of justice that I was supposed to leave to my sister to handle. It was the smart thing to do. She'd as much as told me she had things under control and that she needed me out of it. Posh was not just smart and skilled, she had a lot more experience than I did and going against her request was ridiculous.

So why then was I still thinking about it when I alighted from Pennywhistle outside of Leeth Lacebow's cobbler shop instead of doing what I could to get it out of my mind and go back to the very life that I'd chosen for myself?

I didn't even want to be a Guild investigator.

Leeth greeted me with a bow as I entered, the pixies tinkling their welcome from the back as they carried my new boots forward, both of them beaming at me in their eager delight. It took a lot to stuff down my unhappiness, to sit and allow Leeth to take my old and tired boots away, to admire the new and truly beautiful pair Thrix and Rox had built for me, though I mustered enthusiasm at last as the fitted soles hugged my feet.

The scrolling etchwork in the dark green leather really was exceptional, thick treads perfect for life on the road, the heavy lacing up the back making the fit adjustable depending on my clothing and the padding inside balanced perfectly to the shape of my feet. Both pixies showered the boots with sparkles of their magic, pink and blue, when I finished trying them on, sealing in the shape and the power they'd embedded in the leather.

"Guaranteed for three turnings," Leeth said, flashing his blunt, wide teeth in a big smile as the pixies nodded their agreement.

"Excellent work," I said, handing over the small pouch of coins I'd brought for just this purpose, then adding another gold piece each for the pixies, making sure to deliver them directly to the giggling pair. Leeth made no effort to stop me, watching his staff zip back to work with an indulgent smile. "I'm impressed and will definitely spread the word."

"We're delighted to have such an illustrious member of the Guild use our services," Leeth said. Ah, so he heard who I was, then. "Such a tragedy, the loss of Madam Vorentine."

I didn't want to talk about it, standing and stomping a bit to settle into the boots. Not that it was necessary. They really were the perfect fit. "I'm sure Master Justes will be an excellent replacement." Did I sound sour? I'm sure I did. I made no effort to hide it.

Leeth's pause made me glance up as he shrugged, smile wavering. "The young master will learn, no doubt," he said. "His mother's attempts to teach him the business will hopefully have some influence. But, Master Bard, while perhaps I shouldn't speak ill of the dead, I fear that her faith in him was misplaced and we will again undergo a shift in power in the near future." His concern had me frowning.

"I see," I said. "Thank you for your candor, even

if it's not my business."

"Truly," Leeth said, bobbing a bow and nodding.

I glanced toward the pixies. "You worry another family will try to muscle in?"

"No doubt," Leeth sighed. "They knew better than to try it when Master Balmont passed, since Madam Theringale was already his enforcer. But with her loss and Master Justes' reputation…" the gnome spread his hands. "There will be unrest for a time, loyalties shifting and likely a coup in the next months." He forced a smile. "Not for the first time and certainly not for the last. Though this has been the longest we've been at peace, under the Vorentines, for many years. A shame it couldn't have gone on." He sighed then, carrying the pouch to the counter, adding the contents to his strongbox before whispering magic over it to seal it shut. "Then again, perhaps I'm wrong and Master Justes will prevail. Especially since his young wife, Mistress Darmilla, comes from our previous leader's line."

Excuse me? I leaned on the counter, nodding sagely while an odd little flutter in my chest had me wondering if all of my suppositions might have been utterly and completely off base. "Her family," I said as a prompt.

"Yes, the Callogans," he said, "our fair city's masters, ousted twenty years ago by Balmont Vorentine. I think her hand in marriage was part of the deal struck to ensure the changeover in power. Though," he frowned then as he thought about it, "she left the city after her family was… well.

Removed." Eliminated? "She only returned to us six months ago when the marriage was completed."

So many facts. Not one of the Vorentines chose to share any of it, not even Justes. "Thank you, Leeth," I said, my mood no longer in the doldrums but my anxiety now at full throttle. "You've been more than helpful."

"Good day to you, Master Bard," he said as I hurried out.

*Posh.* I sent a tight message to my sister as I swung up onto Pennywhistle, my horse snorting at my tense vibration.

*Elora*, she sent back, *what is it?*

I need you to look into something for me. I made the request that had her pausing, though not in resistance. I felt her reaching out to someone else, heard a murmur in my mind that was her interaction and then braced for the renewed surge when she returned.

*Confirmed*, she sent. Was that a hum of respect and excitement in her magical touch? *Well done, sister.* Posh went silent again, vibration joined by several others that I recognized as feralfolk—likely Lans and Lire—before she returned. *I'm on my way back*, she sent. *I need to clear this with the Guild first. Considering the situation, this has to be official. Wait for me.*

I was going to. I swear I intended to do just that. But Pennywhistle had already carried me in the direction of the Vorentine estate and I was even now approaching the front gate.

*I'll see you at the house*, I sent and this time it was my

turn to cut my sister off. Like it or not, Guild or not, I was going to see this through and if Posh had an issue, well.

So be it.

"Elora," she breathed. "Look out!"

I turned even before she'd finished, many things happening at once. First, her adventuring friends had begun to recover, scrambling to their feet and running for the exit. Second that the giant shape heading for me wasn't ambling at all, but coming at a pace that meant imminent attack, my second of the day that I might not survive.

"Fig, go!" I pushed her behind me, gathering my thin magic around me while I felt Thune's mind reach for mine.

*ELORA*. His Light burst through me. *I HAVE YOU*.

As he erupted like a flaming dragon from inside me to challenge the charging troll.

## CHAPTER TWENTY-SEVEN

The guards didn't want to let me in. I didn't give them a choice, not above bullying, throwing my badge and weight around until they let me through. I abandoned my horse at the front door, though he was happy enough to graze on the lush front lawn so I didn't worry about him as I strode to the massive entry and pushed my way inside.

The little serving girl took one look at me and squeaked in fear while I scowled back at her.

"Master Justes," I snapped. "Where is he?"

"His quarters, Master Bard," the girl said.

I knew where that was already and didn't waste time stomping my way there. Nor did I knock when I reached it, though someone had magicked the entry shut.

With rogue power. More specifically, an assassin subspell. Good thing bard music trumped it, a song I hummed shattering the softly applied shield meant only for those without power, meant to prevent anyone from accidentally opening the way, not to keep a fully-trained magic user out.

A massive mistake that the assassin I was hunting would regret.

I found her trying to smother him with a pillow, Darmilla's snarl of fury at my appearance unsurprised.

"Step away," I said, noting the carafe next to the bed, the half-empty glass. Whatever plan she'd had to kill Justes went out the window with my arrival, no doubt, her desperate attempt to smother him before escaping obvious. Since she was no longer dressed in a gown at all, her hair now slicked back into a tight bun and her small, thin body sheathed in assassin's black leather. "This is an unauthorized assignment, Darmilla."

"Stay out of it, Yestervere," she snarled from where she crouched on the bed, kneeling on his chest. Justes struggled a little, so I knew he was still alive, but whatever was in that glass next to him likely had enough venilisk in it to immobilize him. Meant to kill him, of course.

"I can't do that," I told her. "You're under arrest for the murder of Balmont Vorentine, Theringale Vorentine and the attempted murder of Justes Vorentine." So there.

"He should already be dead," she snarled, looking down at him. "I underestimated how much venom I needed. The wretched sot's alcohol addiction made him resistant." She shuddered. "I let my emotions get in the way. I know better." When she met my eyes again, hers were cold and grim. "It won't happen again." With deliberate intent, she leaned forward while still staring me down, the pillow compressing further.

I had a song ready, an old battle ballad, the tale of a young wizard faced with impossible odds who'd raised a massive boulder from the ground and smashed an attacking front line of a goblin army, saving his prince and winning the battle. All of which lent my magic the energy to lift the intent assassin from her husband's faintly struggling form and hold her as he gasped for air.

Justes coughed as he rolled over, Darmilla writhing as she fought against my music. Her assassin's magic cut through my tune, dropping her to the floor as the last notes jarred together when she interrupted.

"You shouldn't have interfered," she said, spinning on me, crouching with both hands spread wide.

"Don't even think about it," I said. "You're in enough trouble as it is, Darmilla. The assassin's order deal very harshly with members who go against their rules." Even more so than any others and for obvious reasons. Having assassins go off book without consequences would mean chaos to the structure of the Guild and her superiors would deal succinctly with her in order to maintain their own ability to continue as an order. "You're messing with the very balance of the Guild," I said.

"This would have been dealt with," she said. "With no one the wiser."

"Don't blame me for your terrible life choices," I said.

"I don't," she said in that same icy voice, jabbing a finger at her husband who was now sitting up, bleary but conscious. "I blame him and his family."

"For destroying yours," I said. "I know all about it, Darmilla. How your bloodline ruled here before the Vorentines."

"*Do* you," she said. "Do you also know that Balmont Vorentine was my father's lieutenant and trusted advisor who betrayed him and displaced him?" She'd begun to lose her cold calculation, sliding back into the emotional state she'd regretted just moments ago. "Or that Father promised me to Justes—sealed with a magical contract—before Balmont stabbed him in the back? Mother and I fled, but she died broken and miserable only weeks later. I was forced into a choice at five years old, Elora." She used my first name like we were old friends. "I could walk away and start over. Or."

"Join the assassin's order," I said.

She shrugged. "Father always called me precocious," she said. "And far smarter than a child that age should have been. I understood what was at stake. When the recruiter came to the orphanage, I *volunteered.*" Darmilla's hold over her feelings was fully gone now, hate spewing along with her words. "I planned to spend the rest of my life killing for the

Guild to feed my need for vengeance. It should have been enough."

"Why did you come back?" She could have stayed clear of Vorentine. Surely, her oath to the assassins would have canceled out the marriage contract's magic? She could have found a way to be free of the horrible hurt she wore so distinctly on her young face.

"The order," she said, voice dropping as she turned and stared at Justes. He stared back, blinking at her and then at me, clearly still under the poison's influence. "His request for his parents' assassination. I knew then I had a chance to end it all. I reached out to Balmont and reminded him of the agreement he'd made with my father. I had to shed my oath to reclaim the contract's magic." I'd been right, then. What lengths she went to for her revenge. "I returned here and married this useless piece of humanity." She gestured absently at her husband who gurgled something neither of us understood. Darmilla shrugged and met my eyes again, draining of that hate and settling into amused fury. "I took the traitor's life shortly after my wedding, leaving the poison in his son's possession."

"But no one suspected it was murder," I said.

She didn't seem to mind. "Of course not," she said. "I still had Theringale to kill." She scowled then, hands fisting at her sides as she dropped out of her fighting stance. "She was wary, though. Careful."

"It took six months to get her alone," I said.

Darmilla's dark eyes narrowed. "I finally had to force the issue," she said. "Your arrival made me realize that Guild interference might be imminent. That someone might uncover I'd once been part of the assassin's order." Her scowl returned. "Of course, I knew who you were, Elora Yestervere. But I didn't know you weren't undercover." She tsked at that. "Had I realized you were simply playing at being a bard and not tracking me as I suspected, I wouldn't have risked what I did. My fault."

Now I understood even more. "You thought I was here to bring you back," I said.

Darmilla's faint nod was irritated. "A natural assumption I should have confirmed," she said with grudging agreement.

I'd unwittingly triggered events that led to murder and now I really regretted coming to Vorentine. "Theringale didn't know about the request Justes made, did she?"

"Of course not," Darmilla said as Justes twitched, one hand reaching out toward her before it fell back beside him, his body still fighting the venom. "I needed the means to frame him," she jerked her head toward her husband. "That way, when I killed him it would look like he died of suicide over regret at murdering his own parents." She shrugged. "Easy enough to falsify Theringale's signature. And his on the note I planned to leave."

She thought it all through, hadn't she? "I have to take you in now, Darmilla," I said.

"You and what backup?" She arched an eyebrow at me. "Your sister is back at the Guild with her little pets and your gnome friend is nowhere in sight. Or that rogue friend of yours for that matter." She advanced a step, slow and threatening. "I'll be long gone by the time they find you."

"And hunted for the rest of your life," I said, already preparing a song. I knew the exact one to use, too. My brother inspired it.

"I'll just have to deal with that when the time comes," Darmilla said. "Or, you could let me go." Was that a plea in her voice? She hesitated before speaking again. "I was a child," she said. "This family took mine from me and left me nothing but the need for vengeance. Surely, you understand that."

"I do," I said. "But we don't make the rules, Darmilla." Posh's reminder came to me despite myself. That being part of the Guild meant following their edicts, like it or not. And as much as I railed against such controls, chose a life of independence over bowing and scraping to authority, I had to admit this was the very reason that such rules existed. "I just have to live with them."

She acted without warning, but I already knew what she had planned, her hands extending toward me, sharp claws extending from her gloved fingertips. One scratch would mean my death, I had no doubt. Would have, if not for Thune.

His song, the Paladin's March of Light and Liberty, began with a massive single note that hit like a beam of brilliance, usually accompanied by a choir of voices and a full orchestra, as was fitting my larger-than-life brother and the song that celebrated his most heralded act. His epic battle with the Demon God Smote ended in a permanent gateway to Hel guarded by Thune's original regiment to ensure no other evil ever emerged.

But it began with my brother's battle cry. And a burst of Light like no other.

Darmilla cried out when the room flooded with brilliance, Justes gurgling as he dove for cover, while that giant sound I mustered rocked the entire house, the blaze of my brother's glory blasting the assassin back and crushing her against the far wall.

It only lasted a moment, unlike Thune's original attack. I didn't need to sustain it to succeed. Darmilla was not Demon God, only a broken and grieving young woman bent on revenge, after all.

And I was just a bard who had a lot of thinking to do.

# CHAPTER TWENTY-EIGHT

My *song?* Thune's excitement made my head hurt as he repeated himself yet again. *You used* my *song to defeat her?*

Posh grinned at me, our sister sipping her glass of red wine while the taproom's activity went on around us. I tried to fight the eye roll that arose, my brother's enthusiasm expected, but still a lot.

*I can't wait to tell Mother and Father,* Thune sent. *Love you, Els! Love you, Posh.* He added that almost as an afterthought and then was gone, our sister winking at me with a fake grimace. Thune might have been the leader of the Light and Liberty Paladin order, but he was still a kid at heart.

"I guess you're the favorite now," she said.

"As if," I said. "You know he thinks you're the

best."

"Well, he's not wrong." She arched an eyebrow and then laughed. "I'm really glad we got this chance to work together, Elora. Even if just once."

"Me too," I said, looking down into my own tankard. "You know, I misjudged you, Posh, and I need you to know it." Confession time at last, now that all was said and done. "You're amazing at what you do, of course. Everyone knows it. But this is the first time I've allowed myself to see you as anything but the legend."

She immediately grasped my wrist, her face settling into a sad and anxious expression that only reinforced what I'd just said. "Elora," she whispered. "I'm your sister. I'm just out here doing what I was meant to do. I'm not perfect, you know."

I grinned. "Yes, you are," I said. And laughed. "But I finally feel like I can keep up."

She didn't join in my joke, shaking her head. "You are the best of us, little sister," she said with such intensity that my chuckle faded and my heart sped up. "Thune and I have always known it. Mother, Father. All of us." Posh sighed as she sat back, letting me go. "It broke our hearts when you chose to leave us. But I get it." Her dark blue eyes were full of love when she met my gaze again. "You've become so much more, even, with this time to grow. Now, I wonder if anything will ever stop you." She finally grinned. "You have your own epic adventures ahead, sister, like it or not. Just do me a favor and invite me along more often?" Her wistful request left me flabbergasted.

Fig appeared with a tankard, sitting down and interrupting before I could respond. Posh tossed back her wine, kissing the top of the gnome's head before waving to me and leaving the tavern, gone but not really.

My little friend grinned at me, that smile fading as mine had not too long ago. "Are you all right? What did she say?"

"Nothing," I told my oldest friend. "Are you ready to go in the morning?"

She hesitated, then sagged over her tankard. "There's a team heading into the Everwilding," she said. "I was asked to go."

There was no way I was standing between her and adventure, not now. "Be careful and courageous," I said, saluting her as anxiety clenched inside me.

"Elora." She fixed me with her pale, green eyes. "I've been a jerk." I tried to argue but she waved that off. "Listen, please." I nodded and sat back, waiting for her to go on. It took a deep breath before she did. "You've been the best friend," she said, voice now thick and making me teary in turn, "putting up with me and my shenanigans. I know I'm not a great warrior." She eye rolled and laughed a little. "And I've been an arrogant sot since my last campaign. I know you're worried I'm going to take stupid chances and do ridiculous things and get myself killed." She sighed heavily. "I might," she nodded then. "But it won't be on you. And I have to stop trying so hard to impress you when that's not necessary."

Wait, impress me? I thought about Darmilla, how

I'd triggered her downfall without knowing and refused to be that person for my best friend. "Fig," I choked. Because hadn't I just had this conversation with my sister?

Yes, yes, I had. Did I have influence over others I wasn't expecting? Apparently. Time to take responsibility for that. I wasn't just a bard. I was my mother's daughter, my father's. My impressive siblings' sister. Like it or not. What I did had consequences and I would never get to be ordinary.

Was it time to let go of that desire once and for all?

"I'm not you," Fig said, sitting up straighter. "I'm Fig Marigold, not a Yestervere, as much as I've wished my whole life I was. But I do promise you I'll do everything in my power to stay alive, safe and make you proud of me, no matter what." Tears trickled down her cheeks, paired with the ones I was now weeping, both of us grinning at one another like fools. "Okay?"

I clinked tankards with her. "I know you will," I said. "I'm already proud, Fig."

She beamed at me. "Just promise me you'll hold off on another investigation until I get back."

I groaned at that, though in good jest as she giggled. "For a long time to come," I said. "At least, that's the hope." With Darmilla in the hands of her order and likely about to see her end, I'd been surprised when Justes appeared to have chosen to sober up and take control of his family's business, his announcement just this morning to the city stating just that. With Racheff and Yarra at his side—imagine that duo running the show?—I wondered how long the young Vorentine's rule would last.

I'd find out the next time I came through here, I guess.

Fig finished her drink and left me with a hug, heading out to join her new company while I tried to pay for the drinks.

"Not a copper," Soama and Hathin told me, the wife of the pair gesturing at the overflowing taproom. "Never again, either, Bard Tune. You come to Vorentine, you stay with us like family."

Of course, I sang them a set. Okay, two. Fine, three, but who was counting?

It meant a late departure the next morning, one that had Pennywhistle sighing sadly over since we were heading out alone.

That was, until we reached the crossroads and I debated my course. Continue on past Vorentine into the thinner populated section under the mountains? Or turn back and head for Yinderfell and a visit with my family? I was craving their company, I found, and wondered at this shift in myself.

As someone shivered out of stealth from where she sat on the crossing sign, perched and watching.

"Hello, Mellie," I said, not surprised to find her there.

"Elora," the master rogue said. "I wanted to explain."

"There's nothing to explain," I said. "I hear you made a special request of the rogue academy for Ferrick's reinstatement."

She shrugged. "If he fails out this time, he's on his own," she growled. "You heard Pim's set up?"

Justes had been good to his word, drunken or not, and had granted his half-brother Ferrick's portion of the estate. Likely to shed the agony of the geas, but I chose to give him the benefit of the doubt. At least it meant Pim had a soft place to land and that Ferrick would, too, if his dismal track record with the rogues followed a predictable path.

"I wish her well," I said. "What's next for you?"

She shrugged, hopping down from the signpost. "Reassigned back to the academy," she said with a faint grimace. "Posh's idea. She seems to think I need more structure and that teaching others might give it to me."

That made me laugh. "Good luck with that." It might work and then again, Mellie's independence might actually create problems for the academy. Not on me and I had to believe my sister knew what she was doing.

Though even Posh was open to emotional influence, I now knew. So we'd see, wouldn't we?

Mellie squinted up at me. "You too, Elora," she said. "I mean it. Good luck. I have a feeling things are about to change for you and not in the way you expect." She shivered a little, rubbing at her upper arms with both hands. "My grams was a witchwoman," she said, "who had the Sight. Sometimes, she whispers to me still." Her gray eyes met mine again, intense and narrow. "She's whispering to me now. About you." She looked behind her, the path to Yinderfell raising her eyebrow. "That way lies your Fate."

I tried not to let her warning get to me. It wasn't the first time a Yestervere had that kind of precursor take aim, after all. Except, it had meant the beginning of epic struggles for my parents and my siblings that led to legends and songs and fame.

Something I'd avoided up until now. So, was I ready for my own story to evolve?

"Take care," she said, turning and striding away, taking the well-traveled route. The one that her ghostly ancestor foretold.

I turned away and clucked to Pennywhistle. Mellie's warning made my mind up for me. I loved my family. But the hesitation I still felt at accepting that path was all the truth I needed.

"Mountains it is," I told my horse, grinning into the breeze. "Let's see if we can put off Fate a little longer."

My horse snorted his agreement as he set out on the road, patient as I hummed a tune about the joy of brand-new boots.

Ready for more? Book three is coming soon!
Stay tuned (pun intended!) for more
**Elora Tune: Bard at Large Fantasy Cozies!**

### #3 The Sorcerer Sonata

# AUTHOR NOTES

My very dear reader,

Are you having fun with Elora? I am, which is why I'm already diving into book three, *The Sorcerer Sonata*, with book four, *The Necromancer Nocturne*, right on its heels. My delight in mixing fantasy and cozies hasn't faded. Elora's world is vast and there's so much to explore, including the suggestion she just dropped on me that there's a chance down the road she just might have an adventure with the entire Yestervere clan in an epic showdown that's giving me goosebumps.

But not yet. First, she has to deal with a music festival, a stray zombie outbreak and her own desire to remain independent. Want to find out how that goes? Stay (literally) tuned!

As always, thank you for reading. It is my eternal wish that you stay safe and heathy out there in these most interesting of times. Happy reading, escaping and being you.

Best,
Patti

# ABOUT THE AUTHOR

EVERYTHING YOU NEED TO know about me is in this one statement: I've wanted to be a writer since I was a little girl, and now I'm doing it. How cool is that, being able to follow your dream and make it reality? I've tried everything from university to college, graduating the second with a journalism diploma (I sucked at telling real stories), am an enthusiastic improv performer (if you've never tried it, I highly recommend making things up as you go along as often as possible) and I get to teach and perform with an amazing group of women I adore. I've even been in a Celtic girl band (some of our stuff is on YouTube!) and was an independent filmmaker (go check out the Lovely Witches Club). My life has been one creative thing after another—all leading me here, to writing books for a living.

Now with multiple series in happy publication, I live on beautiful and magical Prince Edward Island (I know you've heard of Anne of Green Gables) with my multitude of pets.

I love-love-love hearing from you! You can reach me (and I promise you, I'll always message back) at patti@pattilarsen.com. And if you're eager for your next dose of Patti Larsen books (usually about one release a month) come join my mailing list! All the best up and coming, giveaways, contests and, of course, my observations on the world (aren't you just dying to know what I think about everything?) all in one place:

http://bit.ly/PattiLarsenEmail.

Last—but not least!—I hope you enjoyed what you read! Your happiness is my happiness. And I'd love to hear just what you thought. A review where you found this book would mean the world to me—reviews feed writers more than you will ever know. So, loved it (or not so much), your honest review would make my day. Thank you!